Love Across Borders

CHARLES E. CRAVEY

IN HIS STEPS PUBLISHING

ISBN: 978-1-58535-069-8 (Paperback)

ISBN: 978-1-58535-070-4 (Kindle)

Library of Congress Catalog Number: 2025912163

Published by In His Steps Publishing, Statesboro, Georgia, USA.

Contents

This book is lovingly dedicated to
all missionaries who make daily sacrifices
for the Lord Jesus Christ and His Kingdom!
May your numbers increase!

Prologue

The love that Harold and Mary shared lasted a lifetime. From that first meeting on Hickory Street, Harold knew that they were destined to be together and share their love with people around the world.

What began as a youthful romance blossomed into a lifelong journey of mission work, taking them across Cambodia, India, Suriname, and Guyana. Through their unwavering commitment to God, they built a career devoted to service, touching countless lives along the way.

Their love transcended borders, reaching hearts in every land they were called to serve. Along this journey, they were blessed with two remarkable children, each growing into leaders, carrying forward the legacy of faith and dedication.

The steadfastness of their devotion remained pure and unwavering, a beacon of inspiration to all who encountered them.

May their numbers continue to grow!

The Rev. Dr. Charles E. Cravey
June 2025, Statesboro, Georgia

CHAPTER ONE

September Morn

O n a crisp September morning, the world came alive as I caught my first glimpse of Mary Rhyne, a captivating presence just a stone's throw away on Hickory Street. Walking alongside my mother's Boykin Spaniel, I suddenly spotted her in her front yard, dressed in a cheerleading ensemble, effortlessly perfecting her graceful moves. With her golden hair gleaming in the sunlight and her radiant beauty, she was nothing short of mesmerizing. Little did I know then that Mary was not only a former cheerleader from her previous high school, but also preparing to try out for our team—an exciting prospect that promised to elevate our squad to new heights!

Her laughter wafted through the air, a captivating melody that danced effortlessly on the gentle breeze.

From my vantage point, I found myself utterly entranced by her presence, overwhelmed by the vibrant energy she radiated. It was as if the very world around her transformed, each moment sparkling with an enchanting touch of magic. Her presence completely captivated me!

Mary glanced up from her routine, a bright smile spreading across her face. "Hey there, kid! Why don't you bring your little friend over? I love dogs!"

I hesitated for a moment before nodding. "Sure. Fluffy's always excited to meet new people."

As I approached, I couldn't help but admire her effortless movements—years of practice evident in every step. "By the way, your cheerleading skills are amazing. You make it look easy."

Mary laughed, brushing a strand of golden hair behind her ear. "Thanks! Cheerleading has always been my thing. Back home in Raleigh, I was on the team. I'm hoping to make the squad here too."

I smiled. "You'll definitely make it. I don't think our team has seen anyone quite like you."

Her eyes sparkled. "You're sweet. I'm Mary Rhyne, by the way. Just moved here with my family. What's your name? And, of course, tell me all about this adorable pup!"

"I'm Harold Brown," I said, adjusting Fluffy's leash. "We live just down the block. And Fluffy? She's the best company you could ask for."

"Well, Harold Brown," Mary said playfully, gently scratching behind Fluffy's ears. "I'd love to have a friend here. Do you think you could be my first?"

The request caught me off guard, but it was easy to answer. "Absolutely! I'd love that."

Her smile deepened. "That means a lot. So, what grade are you in?"

"Sophomore," I said. "I could show you around the school on your first day if you'd like."

"That sounds amazing, Harold. I'd really appreciate that."

Fluffy wiggled excitedly as Mary bent down to pet her. "She's the cutest little thing!" Then she gestured down the street. "How about a walk? You can tell me more about life in this town."

Walking beside her, I felt the unfamiliar excitement of something new—something promising.

Our destinies intertwined more often after that fateful day, as though the universe had orchestrated our lives to merge seamlessly. Mary possessed a beauty that was only matched by her incredible kindness. Her smile and words of encouragement were like sunlight breaking through the clouds, illuminating the hearts of those around her. She had an extraordinary gift for making everyone feel uniquely valued, her authentic warmth beckoning people to her as irresistibly as moths to a flame. My parents embraced Mary whole-heartedly, seeing in her a rare spirit worth cherishing, while her parents, though initially hesitant, gradual-ly came to recognize the bond we shared.

Mary and I quickly forged an unbreakable bond, exchanging stories and laughter beneath the stun-ning tapestry of autumn leaves. Her vibrant spirit was truly contagious; no matter how dreary a day might seem, Mary's enthusiasm and positivity would infuse it with light. She was not just a friend but a force of nature—a whirlwind of joy and kind-ness who left an impression on everyone fortunate enough to cross her path. With Mary by my side, everyday moments turned into cherished memories, and her unwavering zest for life inspired everyone around her to embrace each day with the same fer-vor.

I never considered myself a sports enthusiast, yet that year, I found myself at every home football game, compelled by my unwavering support for Mary. Each time she approached me after the game, wrapping me in a warm hug, I felt like the king of the world. Her presence was electrifying.

She also attended my science competition, where her encouragement meant everything to me. Thanks to her belief in my work, I clinched first place with my project, "Giving Water to the Needy," which highlighted the critical need for water wells in underserved regions and outlined practical solutions for addressing this pressing issue. The way she listened, genuinely captivated by my research, fueled my passion and emboldened my message. Her support didn't just inspire me; it transformed my experience into something unforgettable.

With Mary as my guide, I discovered the transformative power of friendship and the incredible beauty of viewing life through a lens of optimism and hope. She showed me that life is a thrilling adventure meant to be embraced wholeheartedly and fearlessly. As the seasons shifted around us, our friendship flourished, becoming a living testament to the profound connections that arise when two souls truly recognize and nurture the light within each other.

As summer dawned and the new school year approached, the Rhyne family made their way to Webster, settling into the quaint yet timeworn Pritchard house, which had stood empty for over a year. Claude Rhyne, Mary's father, was set to take on the pivotal role of plant manager at the renowned electrical manufacturing facility in town—a key player in supplying parts across the globe. I was genuinely enthusiastic to delve into his work and learn about the fascinating world of electrical manufacturing. Meanwhile, Lisa Rhyne, Mary's mother, was preparing for an exciting new chapter as a second-grade teacher at Webster Elementary School, ready to inspire the next generation of learners come fall.

As the new school year dawned, an electric sense of excitement coursed through me, heightened by the thrill of reconnecting with familiar faces and the prospect of meeting new friends. Webster High was a hive of activity, buzzing with the vibrant energy of students embracing the dynamic rhythm of classes, sports, and social events. The hallways pulsed with animated chatter and laughter, each corner of the school brimming with the potential for unforgettable experiences and lasting friendships. This wasn't just another school year; it was a promising adventure waiting to unfold.

As I made my way through the bustling crowd of students on that first day, my eyes quickly found Mary, surrounded by her cheerleading teammates who had embraced her enthusiastically during tryouts. It was impossible to miss her; her cheerleading uniform radiated a vibrant spirit that complemented the glowing smile on her face. Mary didn't just exude confidence; she embodied it, paired with a warmth that drew others in. These remarkable qualities made her not just a natural leader, but a truly magnetic presence in any gathering, someone who could easily inspire those around her. The cheerleaders had been asked to do a short performance at the morning assembly, so they had dressed for the occasion.

As our eyes locked across the bustling hallway, she waved at me with that same infectious enthusiasm that had always drawn me in. With each step I took toward her, a warm sense of familiarity enveloped me amidst the wave of unknown faces. Mary graciously introduced me to her friends, and in an instant, we were immersed in lively conversation, exchanging our aspirations and dreams for the upcoming year. It felt not just like a meeting but the beginning of something special, a connection that promised the thrill of shared experiences ahead.

I offered a friendly smile. "Would you like me to show you around, Mary? I'd be happy to give you a tour."

Mary chuckled, shaking her head slightly. "That's really kind of you, Harold, but the girls already took me on an amazing tour. I think I've got the layout down." She gave a reassuring look. "But if I do get lost, you'll be the first person I turn to for help."

As the weeks went by, an undeniable connection formed between Mary and me during those fleeting moments between classes and at lunch. We exchanged stories about our classes and teachers, diving deep into the whirlwind of teenage life together. Mary's vibrant optimism was truly contagious, transforming even the most ordinary moments into cherished memories that I knew I would hold onto for a lifetime.

One sunny afternoon, as we relaxed together on the lush green lawn, Mary opened about her aspiration to become a journalist. Her deep-seated love for storytelling and her natural curiosity about the world fueled her ambition. You could feel her passion radiating from her, and it was impossible not to be inspired by her steadfast commitment to create meaningful change through the power of her words. Mary spoke eloquently about her desire to uncover significant stories, to illuminate the untold narratives woven into the fabric of everyday life. Her fervor was infectious, igniting a sense of purpose in those who listened.

In those moments, I found myself truly captivated by Mary—not merely for her striking beauty and vibrant charisma, but for her unwavering ambition and the profound depth of her character. She was more than a friend; she was a beacon of inspiration, urging me to dream bigger and welcoming the boundless possibilities of the future with enthusiasm. Each moment we shared that year felt like a treasure, filled with promise and unforgettable experiences. My admiration for her only grew stronger, reminding me of the incredible impact she had on my life.

As the school year unfolded, our friendship blossomed into something truly remarkable, demonstrating the profound strength found in shared dreams and the deep connections born from laughter and mutual understanding. Together, we faced the difficulties of high school life, our friendship serving as a steadfast anchor in the turbulent seas of adolescence. It was this unwavering bond that not only helped us celebrate our victories but also supported us through the challenges, proving that together, we could navigate anything that came our way.

One day, Mary turned to me with a curious smile. "Harold Brown, what do you see yourself becoming when you grow up?"

Her question stirred something deep within me, prompting me to reflect on my dreams and aspirations for the future.

I enthusiastically shared my lifelong dream of becoming a missionary in foreign lands. My passion lies in not only sharing my faith but also empowering communities by teaching them innovative practices and enhancing healthcare through modern medicine. I believe that by bridging cultural gaps and providing valuable insights, I can make a meaningful impact on the lives of those I serve.

Mary's eyes widened in surprise. "Wow! I never would've guessed you, Harold Brown, as a missionary!"

I nodded, offering a small smile. "I get that a lot. People usually chuckle when I tell them, but I'm completely serious, Mary. My passion is helping others improve their lives and guiding them toward the love of Jesus Christ."

Mary initially appeared taken aback by my comments, her expression reflecting a moment of uncertainty. However, after a brief pause, she gathered her thoughts and responded thoughtfully.

"Harold Brown," she said, her voice filled with genuine admiration, "that's truly one of the most inspiring things I've ever heard. How do you plan to achieve that?"

"I have an exciting plan in place for my future! Thanks to our church minister, I've connected with Asbury College in Wilmore, Kentucky, where they specialize in training missionaries for the Methodist Church. I'm eager to enroll in their program immediately after graduating high school. This opportunity will not only equip me with the skills I need to make a meaningful impact, but it will also allow me to deepen my faith and serve others in a profound way."

"Absolutely, Harold Brown!" she exclaimed, her enthusiasm palpable. "You can count on me for 100 percent of my steadfast support!"

Beneath the warm, golden hues of autumn, Mary and I forged unforgettable memories that would weave themselves into the fabric of our lives. Together, we navigated the ups and downs of high school, and with a steadfast friend like Mary by my side, I felt invincible. Every challenge became an opportunity, and

I was certain that if we faced them together, there was nothing we couldn't conquer.

By the time we reached eleventh grade, sitting together in class had become a cherished tradition for Mary and me. Every afternoon, we would come together to study, either enveloped in the cozy atmosphere of her home or nestled comfortably in mine. During these sessions, Mary would share her vibrant dreams of becoming an outstanding journalist, longing to explore the world and craft captivating stories. With every moment we spent together, I found myself falling more deeply in love with this incredible girl. I sensed she might have felt something too, but the uncertainty held me back from expressing my feelings. The thought of revealing my heart to her filled me with both excitement and fear.

We are thrilled to share how Mary and her family joined our church community at Christ United Methodist at our invitation. From the very first service, our two families bonded, filling an entire pew with laughter and warmth. My parents and Mary's family quickly became like one big, happy family, discovering a wealth of common interests that drew us even closer. Our connection extended beyond church, as we cheered side by side at football and basketball games.

While I was still learning the ins and outs of the sports, my enthusiasm for our team never wavered, thanks to the joyful camaraderie we shared.

As the sun began its descent towards the horizon during our Junior year, I mustered up the courage to invite Mary to the Junior/Senior Prom. To my delight, she accepted with a beaming smile, and it felt as if the stars had aligned just for us. The thought of dancing together, enveloped in the magic of the moment, filled me with anticipation.

However, as we glided across the dance floor, my clumsiness got the better of me, and I found myself stepping on Mary's toes repeatedly. Each time, I felt a mix of embarrassment and determination to make it up to her, realizing that our connection was far more important than any misstep. This night, with all its awkwardness and joy, would become a defining moment in my young life—a night I would always cherish.

I set out in my mother's trusty old Chevy, with Mary beside me, ready to embrace the magic of the grand Prom. After the celebration, we made our way to the enchanting Wesley State Park, parking by the tranquil lake that reflected the stars above. It was here, amidst the gentle sounds of nature, that we exchanged whispers of our hopes and dreams. I could see the spark of excitement in Mary's eyes, a vivid reminder of the endless possibilities that lay before us as we embarked on our new journeys.

The moonlight danced on the water's surface, casting a silver spell over the scene as we sat together in tranquil silence, the world around us quietly receding into the night. Mary leaned in closer, her hand gently resting on mine—a simple yet powerful gesture that spoke volumes of her encouragement and deep understanding. In that moment, her presence enveloped me like a warm embrace, a comforting reminder that I wasn't alone. I felt an overwhelming sense of gratitude for her steadfast support, a lifeline that grounded me amidst the chaos.

Mary's voice was warm with admiration. "Harold, your courage has always inspired me. You have such a compassionate spirit, and you'll make a profound difference wherever your mission work takes you."

Her words ignited a fire within me, solidifying my determination and filling me with a newfound sense of purpose. As the night wore on, we engaged in deep conversation, envisioning the incredible places I would explore and the enchanting stories she would eventually craft. This exchange of dreams wasn't just a fleeting moment; it fortified our connection and drew us closer together, intertwining our aspirations in a tapestry of shared ambition.

As the stars sparkled overhead, Mary opened about her dreams with a fervor that was truly inspiring. Her passion for storytelling shone brightly as she expressed her commitment to giving a voice to those who are often unheard. Together, we envisioned the thrilling adventures that lay ahead, the obstacles we would overcome, and the meaningful change we aspired to create in the world. That night was filled with hope and endless possibilities, etching a lasting memory in my heart that I will carry with me always.

As the cool night air wrapped around us, a gentle reminder that it was time to head home, I couldn't help but reflect on the unforgettable evening we had shared. Driving through the quiet streets, a profound sense of gratitude washed over me for Mary—an extraordinary girl who had woven herself into the fabric of my life. The journey ahead may be filled with uncertainties, but with Mary by my side, I felt an exhilarating confidence. Together, we were ready to take on whatever the future had in store for us, embracing every twist and turn with open hearts.

In the days that followed, we seized every opportunity to be together, fully embracing each moment before the life-altering changes graduation would bring. Our friendship flourished, evolving into a profound bond that reflected the strength of our shared dreams and unwavering respect for one another. It was a beautiful reminder of how meaningful connections can thrive, even in the face of impending change.

As the school year came to a close, I realized our paths might soon part ways. Yet, I clung to the belief that our bond would remain strong. The journey to Asbury College marks the beginning of an exciting new chapter in our lives, and I am genuinely excited to discover all the possibilities that lie ahead.

As I stood on the brink of the next chapter in my life, I felt the undeniable warmth of that unforgettable lakeside night enveloping me. It was a night filled with whispered dreams exchanged beneath a tapestry of stars, where the promise of a love emerged—one that would forever inspire and elevate my spirit. This memory was not just a fleeting moment; it became the foundation of my journey forward, reminding me of the extraordinary potential that lies in hope and connection.

Mary and I quickly became the talked-about legends of our senior year at Webster High. As the year progressed, she made a pivotal decision to step back from her cheerleading duties, redirecting her energy toward her studies and elevating her GPA. With aspirations of entering the prestigious University of Georgia to pursue a career in journalism, her academic success became not plainly important, but essential serving as the crucial key that would unlock the doors to her dream of becoming a master storyteller.

We both recognized that this year was crucial for our futures, and I couldn't help but admire Mary's unwavering dedication and relentless drive. Amidst her deep dives into textbooks, she radiated a vibrant energy that lit up my life, her passion for learning both infectious and motivating. Together, we became each other's pillars of support, finding comfort in our shared study sessions and those rare moments of reprieve when we escaped into the worlds created by books and films. Our movie nights were often filled with powerful tales of mission work or the introspective journeys found in journaling, each film enriching our minds and strengthening our bond even more.

As the last few months of high school approached, we were swept up in a whirlwind of exams, college applications, and bittersweet goodbyes. Yet amidst this chaotic mix, there was a palpable sense of anticipation. Our journey at Webster High had been nothing short of transformative, molding us into the confident individuals we were destined to become. Equipped with newfound courage and a steadfast conviction, we stood ready to embrace the world ahead.

On a beautiful, brisk morning in late spring, Mary received her acceptance letter from the University of Georgia—a moment filled with joyous disbelief and an exhilarating rush of plans for the future. This was not just an acceptance; it was the realization of her dream. I wholeheartedly believe that Mary will thrive in this new academic environment, as her unwavering passion for storytelling will undoubtedly steer her towards success in her studies and beyond. The possibilities ahead are limitless, and her journey is just beginning.

As the reality of our upcoming separation loomed before us, it was a moment filled with both sadness and hope. We recognized the importance of cherishing every remaining moment together, fully committed to making it count. We made a heartfelt promise to stay connected and to support one another, no matter the miles between us. Deep down, we believed that our bond was strong enough to withstand any distance, and we were determined to ensure our friendship not only endured but thrived.

As graduation day drew near, an exhilarating yet nerve-wracking energy enveloped us all. The ceremony transformed into a vibrant tapestry of caps soaring, gowns flowing, and beaming smiles that lit up the crowd, punctuated by bittersweet farewells. Standing together, Mary and I gazed toward an uncertain future, fueled by hope and immense gratitude for our journey. We knew deep in our hearts that the bonds we forged during our time together would be a lasting treasure, forever woven into the fabric of our lives.

As we tossed our caps high into the air, marking both an end and a thrilling new beginning, an overwhelming sense of peace washed over me. Although our paths were set to diverge, the dreams we had nurtured together would forever bind us in spirit. This moment was more than just a celebration of our accomplishments—it was a powerful reminder of the strength of our friendship and the lasting influence of the invaluable moments we shared. Together, we had forged memories that would inspire us as we stepped bravely into the future.

Our church hosted an extraordinary celebration for Mary, me, and three other deserving graduates of our church, and it was truly an unforgettable experience! The event was beautifully organized, featuring a delightful meal and an array of delicious treats to enjoy afterward. Pastor Henry Proctor took a moment to share inspiring words about our future aspirations and the exciting journey ahead. He then invited us to express our thoughts and gratitude, adding a delicate touch to the occasion. We had a fantastic time, and we felt incredibly appreciated for all the support our church has shown us. It was a remarkable testament to the love and encouragement within our community, and we couldn't be more grateful for this celebration in our honor!

With hearts brimming with hope and the world unfolding before us, we boldly embarked on the next chapter of our lives, eager to seize the exciting adventures that awaited us.

Chapter Two

Bound by the Stars

D uring our four years in college, the cherished moments spent together in Webster during spring and fall breaks, as well as Thanksgiving and Christmas, became the highlights of our lives. Each visit deepened our connection and allowed our love to grow. Mary shared the challenges she faced in her classes, and I could relate to her struggles. I, too, shared my own difficulties in theology, strengthening our bond beyond the pressures of our coursework. These gatherings weren't just reunions; they were essential reminders of the strength of our relationship and the support we offered each other during our challenges.

As spring neared during our senior year, Mary and I eagerly looked forward to graduation from our respective schools, bubbling with excitement and anticipation for the future. Mary was on the brink of earning her journalism degree at the University of Georgia, a crucial step toward her dream career in storytelling and uncovering the truth. At the same time, I was about to receive my diploma and commission from Asbury, ready to embark on a significant adventure. My future was thoughtfully planned out—a mission field assignment that would take me to distant lands, immersing me in new cultures and experiences far beyond the comforts of home. This was more than just a change; it marked the start of an extraordinary journey that would profoundly shape our lives in ways we had yet to envision.

As I stood on the brink of the future, I felt the profound weight of change pressing down on me. After graduation, we reconvened in Webster, our beloved childhood town, where every corner was alive with memories that whispered tales of innocence and growth. The moment Mary saw me, her face lit up with uncontainable joy, her vibrant enthusiasm as infectious as ever. She had landed a highly sought-after role as a beat reporter for the Atlanta Constitution—a dream she had tirelessly worked to attain. In just a week, she would set off for Atlanta, eagerly chasing the stories that ignited her passion and purpose.

I felt a true sense of inspiration listening to her ambitions and dreams. However, when the discussion shifted to my own future, a disquieting sensation started to settle in my chest. I shared the assignment I had received—a call to serve in Cambodia, a country I had explored through my studies but felt so far removed from my familiar life. With my deployment approaching in just a month, the magnitude of this opportunity weighed heavily on me, sparking a mix of excitement and anxiety.

That realization lingered between us, an unspoken understanding that colored every moment we shared. Each silent glance only added to the gravity of our collective awareness—time was slipping away. Resolute in our desire to cherish every instant, we plunged into the joy of being together. Our afternoons flowed seamlessly into twilight walks, where our laughter intertwined with the warm evening breeze and reverberated against the softening sky. We sought solace beneath the oak tree of my youth, a haven steeped in memories. In that sacred space, we reflected on our shared history while wrestling with the uncertainty of the future. Every moment transformed into a cherished keepsake, leaving an everlasting imprint on our hearts as we embraced the beauty of the present.

During one of those peaceful evening strolls, a sudden realization washed over me—an undeniable and profound truth that clamored for recognition. As Mary walked beside me, the setting sun casting a golden halo around her hair, I felt my heart begin to race with excitement. In that instant, the world around us seemed to disappear. I stopped, faced her, and without a moment's hesitation, I leaned in and kissed her, compelled by an irresistible pull I could no longer ignore.

In that instant, everything around us seemed to stand still, as if time had held its breath. Her lips, soft and inviting, carried the burden of countless unexpressed secrets. When we finally separated, her expression was illuminated with pure astonishment, as if she had just stumbled upon a profound revelation.

Mary's playful curiosity radiated as she tilted her head. "Harold Brown, where did that come from?"

A smile crept onto my face, a comforting warmth enveloping my chest. "I felt it was the only decision I could make," I confessed, my voice firm with resolve. "From the very first moment on Hickory Street, I realized I loved you. That feeling hasn't diminished; it remains just as powerful today. We were destined to find each other, that this was always meant to be our journey." I inhaled deeply, then posed the question that weighed most heavily on my heart. "Mary, will you marry me?"

She met my eyes, and it felt as if my words had pierced through to her innermost feelings. Finally, with a calm determination, she murmured, "Harold, I've harbored these feelings for so long. You've been my source of strength, my muse, and my steadfast support. It would be the greatest honor to call you, my husband."

A powerful rush of joy washed over me, a feeling I had never encountered before. As we held each other close beneath the endless starry sky, we exchanged our dreams for the future—images of adventure, a meaningful life, and a love strong enough to withstand any distance we might face. In that instant, I realized we were connected by an unbreakable bond, prepared to tackle whatever challenges awaited us side by side.

In the days following our engagement, a celebration blossomed, uniting our families and friends in eager anticipation. With hearts brimming with excitement, they enthusiastically joined us in organizing the wedding set for a special day in December. Decisions fell into place quickly, fueled by a shared sense of urgency; time was of the essence, yet our love held steady, anchoring us as we embarked on this thrilling journey toward our future together.

As our week together ended, I wandered through the beloved streets of Webster, the town that had shaped our journey. Each structure, every twisting path, and the fresh aroma of rain hanging in the air felt like pieces of a vibrant tapestry crafted from our shared experiences. Yet, as Mary and I prepared to set off on a new adventure, a thrilling wave of anticipation washed over me for the unwritten chapters ahead—exciting moments that neither of us could foresee, just waiting to be revealed.

The wedding is set for Christmas Eve, perfectly aligning with my first furlough in December. In the lead-up to this special day, Mary will be working diligently with our parents in Webster to meticulously plan every aspect of the ceremony. Her commitment and effort are sure to make this event truly memorable.

One evening, while sitting next to Mary on the porch of her family home, the mesmerizing flicker of fireflies lit up the warm Georgia twilight, surrounding us with a mystical radiance. In that tranquil moment, I felt a stirring sense of impending change—an unspoken shift that hung in the air, prompting me to contemplate the journey that lay ahead for us both.

"I despise having to leave so quickly," I confessed, my voice scarcely louder than a whisper.

Mary grasped my hand, her touch firm and comforting. "I understand," she whispered, her eyes steady and sincere. "But this isn't the conclusion—it's merely the start of something extraordinary."

It was a simple declaration, yet it struck a deep chord within me. As I held her hand, I grounded myself in the steadfast reality of her words. Despite the unknowns that awaited us, I felt a strong certainty that Mary and I would tackle this challenge side by side, just as we had overcome every hurdle in the past. Following our wedding in December, Mary would accompany me to Cambodia for our mission, ensuring she obtained her passport and visa before I made my way back to Webster. Together, we were prepared to confront anything that life threw our way.

As we bid our bittersweet farewells to our childhood town, I held Mary's hand tightly, savoring the cherished memories we had built together while looking forward to the exciting possibilities that awaited us. With Mary heading to Atlanta and me beginning my journey to Cambodia, we both carried the hope of new adventures, forever linked by our shared history and the promise of what lies ahead.

With that fresh perspective, I felt an undeniable pull toward Cambodia.

Chapter Three

Cambodia

Aften a month of rigorous study, I finally arrived in Battambang—a town rich in history, alive with energy, and infused with a culture that resonated with every step I took. Coming from a small town in Georgia, the dusty roads and the echoes of ancient temples that surrounded me were captivating. I held on to the steadfast conviction that if God had led me to this extraordinary place, He would also guide me through any challenges that lay ahead.

My journey at the Methodist Center began under the invaluable mentorship of Rupert Foster, a dedicated missionary whose twenty-seven years of service in this vibrant land had made him a wellspring of knowledge and experience. Rupert's calm wisdom, complemented by his occasional light-hearted humor, provided me with much-needed stability as I navigated the whirlwind of colors, sounds, and aromas that is Cambodia.

I was given a very modest room in the back of the Methodist Center. I had a small kitchenette, a single bed, dresser, and a shared bath at the end of the hall. There were two other interns who stayed in separate rooms down the hall and would be invaluable help in my indoctrination. Brad and Charlie had been in Battambang for six months by the time I arrived. They shared with me all things – Cambodia, and I was most thankful. We were immersed daily in the Khmer language and began talking to each other using it.

"Chum reap suor. Neak sok sabai te?" Brad asked me one day. This was the respectful way of greeting someone in Cambodia. We would also learn the traditional "sampeah" gesture by placing our palms together and resting them on our chest and bowing slightly.

"Khnhom sok sabai. Anak ponman," "I am well, thank you," came my response.

This is how we practiced with each other daily. The people among whom we worked with in the villages would daily teach us more of the language and their ways of living. We were being deeply immersed in the culture and life of our people.

Every day, I found myself captivated by the bustling markets, where stalls brimmed with exotic fruits, aromatic spices, and brilliantly colored textiles. The enchanting rhythm of the Khmer language floated through the air, wrapping the experience in a melodic embrace. Here, life unfolded like a rich tapestry—one intricately woven with threads of joy that persist even in the face of adversity.

Charlie asked me one day, "How are things going for you here, Harold?"

"Fine," I answered. "I'm really learning the ropes slowly, but surely."

Brad and Charlie were both so encouraging each day and at night both would lead us in a devotional period. They were both already knowledgeable about Mary and our upcoming wedding and kidded me each day with some smart quip about our relationship. Both Brad and Charlie had dedicated their lives to the ministry and would soon be sent out to start their own churches up in the mountains. The thought of that warmed my heart and it showed their devotion to God's call upon them.

The genuine connections I built with the local community profoundly shaped my journey of healing and growth. Teaching English to neighborhood children became a source of immense joy, particularly when it came to a spirited teenager named Sopheak. His bright, curious eyes and enthusiastic smile transformed every lesson into a shared adventure. One memorable afternoon, as we relaxed under the sprawling branches of an ancient banyan tree, Sopheak opened up about his dream of becoming a teacher. With all the warmth and conviction I could muster, I looked him in the eye and said, "You can achieve anything you set your mind to, Sopheak." In that moment, his hope stirred memories of my own youthful aspirations, bridging our experiences in a powerful reminder that passion knows no boundaries.

Sopheak soon began attending our evening vespers at the Center and grew in his faith with each passing evening. He was eager to learn, and I could see the gleam in his eyes for what he was learning.

During my time in Battambang, I made it a priority to write to Mary as often as possible. Each letter poured forth the vivid tapestry of my experiences—the steadfast spirit of the Cambodian people, the joyful laughter of children, and the serene moments of introspection beneath breathtaking sunsets. Meanwhile, in her letters from Atlanta, where she thrived as a reporter, she shared heartfelt updates and meticulously detailed wedding plans that lifted my spirits during my solitude. Her words served as a lifeline, connecting me to home while inspiring me to face each challenge with courage and determination. Once a month we were each allowed a call home, so I would call Mary and talk to her and asked her to relay any activities to my parents back home in Webster.

One sweltering afternoon, after a day filled with challenging work that left me both satisfied and drained, an unnerving weakness began to creep over me. At first, I dismissed the feverish chills and aching limbs as nothing more than fatigue setting in. However, as dusk descended, my body turned against me in a shocking twist. While I was engaged in a local project, an overwhelming wave of dizziness crashed over me like a relentless tide, and in an instant, I collapsed in front of a growing crowd. I'll never forget Rupert's expression of sheer horror as he rushed to my side, his voice urgent and pleading, begging me to seek immediate medical help.

"Son, I'm calling for an ambulance. You've probably contracted dengue fever, and it can be life-threatening." Rupert was very concerned and wasted no time to secure the help I needed.

In just a few short hours, I found myself confined to a cramped, sterile room in a Phnom Penh hospital. The relentless beeping of monitors and the soft footsteps of the medical staff served as a jarring reminder of the stark reality I was facing, a stark contrast to the vibrant life that thrived just beyond those walls. It wasn't long before I learned the shocking truth: I was grappling with a severe case of dengue fever—a life-threatening infection that had stealthily taken hold. As I lay there in that cold, clinical environment, an intense sense of loneliness washed over me, compounded by a paralyzing fear of confronting death so far away from the comforting embrace of home.

"Rupert, would you pray with me?" I asked.

"Of course I will, Harold," he responded, and layed his hands on my head and offered the sweetest prayer for my recovery of any I had ever heard. I still owe my recovery to both God and Rupert for their faithfulness to me and the mission.

On one of those long, silent nights after Rupert had left, a compassionate nurse entered my room, bringing a flicker of hope with her. Her broken English, laced with a tender accent, wrapped around me like a comforting blanket as she gently placed a cool cloth on my fevered brow. "You're going to beat this, Harold. Rest now—trust us," she whispered, her eyes shimmering with a blend of unwavering determination and deep empathy. In her simple yet powerful gesture, I was transported back to the soothing embrace of my mother during my childhood fevers, allowing me to feel my own vulnerability mingling with an overwhelming sense of gratitude. In that moment, I realized how the caring touch of another could reignite hope even in the darkest of times.

Rupert's daily visits were a breath of fresh air, his voice always a soft murmur filled with reverence as he spoke of life and faith. One memorable day, in the serene stillness of the corridor, he shared a deeply personal story from his youth in Cambodia—a narrative that began in despair but blossomed into hope through relentless perseverance. His words, rich with both sorrow and encouragement, compelled me to face my own painful reality. Though I often felt weak, Rupert's insights reminded me that I was bound to a purpose far greater than myself, igniting a flicker of strength within me that I never knew I possessed.

In the serene moments beside my hospital window, I found myself captivated by a humble lotus pond, bathed in the soft, luminous glow of the moon. As I gazed at those delicate blossoms, I couldn't help but see them as a powerful metaphor for my own journey. Even amidst the murky waters of hardship, extraordinary beauty and profound transformation can emerge. This image became my guiding light—a steadfast reminder that from the depths of suffering, a new strength and clarity can be born. Embracing this vision gave me hope, revealing that renewal is not just a possibility but an inevitable part of life's journey.

With each carefully administered dose of treatment and the untiring kindness from both the locals and my fellow missionaries, the relentless grip of the fever began to loosen. I emerged from my harrowing battle with dengue fever not just battered but profoundly transformed—a living testament to life's fragile beauty and the depth of God's mercy. Every ache and every scar I carry now serve as a powerful reminder to treasure each heartbeat and embrace the gift of life with gratitude.

The news of my long-awaited furlough echoed in my mind like a distant bell, a beacon of hope that promised a longed-for reunion with Mary and the solace of home. As my time in the hospital dwindled, her letter became my sanctuary—a heartfelt tapestry woven with the intricacies of our wedding plans and soothing reassurances that filled my heart with warmth. I treasured those words, clutching them tightly as though they were a lifeline, grounding my spirit and fortifying me as I prepared to leave behind the place that had so profoundly etched itself onto my soul. Following my furlough, Mary would be returning here with me as my wife. Rupert assured me that an apartment behind the Center would be readied for our return. Mary would be helping out at the Center with intakes and documenting our work in all the different villages in the surrounding area.

As the day of my departure dawned, I was swept away by a whirlwind of emotions. On the flight to Atlanta, I sank into deep contemplation, my thoughts drifting back to the lively streets of Battambang, to Sopheak's infectious laughter, and to the profound moments of introspection spent in the hospital under the harsh fluorescent glow. With each line of Mary's letter that I reread, her words resonated within me, intertwining with my heartbeat—a powerful vow that our love would remain a steadfast beacon, illuminating my path despite the miles that lay ahead.

As I stepped off the plane in Atlanta, the cool Georgia air welcomed me like a refreshing embrace, a stark contrast to the stifling humidity of Cambodia. In the bustling arrivals hall, the sight of Mary's radiant smile and her open arms instantly dissolved the weight of my weary journey. In that heartfelt reunion, I experienced not only the physical relief of returning home but also the profound reassurance of a love that had triumphed over the trials of time, distance, and even brushes with mortality. It was a moment that reaffirmed the strength of our bond and the definite warmth of a connection that truly transcends all obstacles.

In the days leading up to our wedding, as we shared quiet moments filled with whispered prayers and intimate conversations over morning coffee, I couldn't help but reflect on every meaningful memory from my time in Cambodia. I replayed the heartfelt discussions with Rupert, the small yet impactful acts of kindness I witnessed in the hospital, and the profound connection I felt with the lotus blooming just outside my window. During these contemplative moments, Mary and I explored the exciting possibility of her joining me on future missions—an idea that sparked both trepidation and an exhilarating sense of hope. With her by my side, the thought of serving together transformed the uncertain path ahead into a shared journey that felt not merely achievable but truly inspiring.

As I prepare to step into the extraordinary moment of our wedding day in Georgia, I hold close the profound mosaic of my experiences in Cambodia—a tapestry woven with threads of pain, hope, and a deep gratitude for life's delicate beauty. The resilient lotus, rising majestically from the depths of murky waters, reflects our journey perfectly: in the face of adversity, it is love and bravery that flourish. Together, we have crafted a story rich with triumph, and I am eager to celebrate this next chapter with you.

This chapter—defined by fire, resilience, and the promise of renewal—stands as an enduring testament to the extraordinary power of hope and the strength found in human connection. I eagerly anticipate a future in which each step, every challenge, and all triumphs further enrich a life steeped in purpose, compassion, and boundless love. Together, let us embrace the journey ahead, knowing that our shared experiences will illuminate the path towards a brighter tomorrow.

Chapter Four

The Grand Wedding

A s the soft light of dawn bathed the rolling hills of Webster, I awoke with a profound certainty— today was the day Mary and I would unite our lives forever. In those peaceful early moments, I took the time to reflect on the incredible journey that led me from the vibrant yet challenging streets of Cambodia to this beautiful occasion in our Southern hometown. Every obstacle I encountered, every heartfelt letter from Mary, and each whispered prayer in solitude played a vital role in shaping my path, steering me toward this sacred day of union. It was not just a moment—it represented the culmination of our love's resilience and the promise of a future woven intricately together.

Mary and I met with Pastor Proctor the evening before to discuss final plans for the ceremony. He also led both of us in an incredibly beautiful, heartfelt prayer. Within hours we would stand before Pastor Proctor, our parents, the congregation, and God to proclaim our love for each other—a most solemn and momentous occasion.

As I drew near to Christ United Methodist Church in the late afternoon, a flurry of nervous excitement stirred within me, intermingling with an overflowing sense of joy that was hard to contain. The church's brilliant white walls and pristine pews radiated a welcoming warmth and reverence as I stepped inside. The gentle, ethereal tones of the organ filled the air, crafting a sacred atmosphere that touched my heart profoundly.

The sweet scent of fresh lilies surrounded me, while the soft chatter of family and friends uplifted my spirit. It was in this moment that I recalled the long nights I had endured in a hospital in Phnom Penh. The stark, cold atmosphere of that sterile space felt distant, eclipsed by the kind words of a compassionate nurse and the steadfast support of Rupert at my side.

Those challenging experiences, though difficult, had cultivated a strength within me, enabling me to fully appreciate this moment with a deep sense of gratitude and purpose. I felt prepared to embrace every precious second of what was to come.

As I stood at the altar with Pastor Proctor and my best man, Sean, my heart raced while I watched Mary walk down the aisle. Clad in a breathtaking cotton gown embellished with delicate lace, she exuded a natural Southern grace that illuminated the soft morning light. With each step she took, vivid memories rushed back to me—our first encounter on that crisp September morning on Hickory Street, the laughter that echoed through our exchanged letters, and the tears that solidified our connection. Each heartbeat served as a powerful reminder of how far we had journeyed, overcoming not only distances but also the emotional barriers that once felt insurmountable. In that moment, I realized we were more than just two individuals; we were the embodiment of a journey forged through love, spirit, and a profound bond.

As Pastor Proctor began the ceremony, his calming and comforting voice filled the sanctuary, fostering an atmosphere rich with warmth and hope. The moment for exchanging vows was approaching, and in that fleeting moment, I pondered the countless challenges I had encountered—from traversing the lively markets of Battambang to braving nights steeped in uncertainty in Cambodia. All these experiences coalesced within me, leading to a heartfelt promise that surpassed both time and hardship. Standing before Mary, who would soon accompany me back to Cambodia, I inhaled deeply and started my vows with the words I had rehearsed tirelessly, each syllable carrying the significance of our shared journey:

"Mary, I vow to love you passionately with every beat of my heart, always standing by your side through the sunniest days and the most challenging nights. I will treasure the remarkable spirit that has guided us through every obstacle, from the lively hustle of Cambodia to the peaceful times we enjoy in Webster. Together, we will navigate life's journey, hand in hand, always united."

As I moved to the next section, a commitment that was supposed to capture all the hope and conviction within me, it hit me—I'd missed an essential word. In that brief instant, a heavy silence fell over the room. I could feel the attention of every eye on me; the warmth of every encouraging smile filled with expectation. Taking a deep breath to steady my nerves, I proclaimed, "I promise to always... stand by your side, to love you passionately and support you in every meaningful way—"

Laughter rippled through the congregation, creating a moment of warmth that united us all. Mary leaned forward, her eyes sparkling with playful affection as she murmured, "I love you, silly." Even Pastor Proctor couldn't suppress a knowing smile that spread across his face. In that brief, beautifully imperfect moment, the heaviness of seriousness faded away, revealing a fundamental truth: true love isn't about perfection; it flourishes in our charming human flaws, reminding us that it is these moments that genuinely connect us.

With a newfound sense of calm, I smiled and proclaimed, "I pledge to cherish the journey of our love, honoring every stumble as an essential part of our remarkable story." My heartfelt and unscripted words resonated with everyone gathered, weaving together humor and profound emotion into the fabric of our vows. In that poignant moment of shared vulnerability, everyone felt the true depth of our commitment, affirming the strength of our bond.

As the ceremony wrapped up, the church resounded with enthusiastic applause and heartfelt cheers, capturing the deep joy that permeated the air. Upon stepping outside, guests found themselves surrounded by the majestic oak trees draped in delicate strands of Spanish moss, all illuminated by the warm embrace of the Georgia sun. Families and friends gathered to celebrate, exemplifying the essence of Southern hospitality. Laughter filled the atmosphere, blending perfectly with the melodic strains of a string quartet, while the joyful clinking of glasses during heartfelt toasts added to the enchanting ambiance, radiating hope and excitement for what lies ahead.

Mary and I took a peaceful stroll along a winding path lined with graceful camellia bushes. Sunlight filtered through the branches, casting a gentle warmth on the ground as we leaned closer together, whispering our dreams and visions for the future. "Each challenge I encountered overseas, Mary, every moment of fear in that hospital, has only led me back to you," I said, softly squeezing her hand. Her eyes glimmered in the soft light as she responded, "And every heartfelt word you've shared has only deepened our unbreakable bond. I stand strong here because I believe in us."

That evening, our celebration flowed into a stunning reception hall, adorned with rustic lanterns, wildflowers, and the warm shimmer of candlelight. The atmosphere buzzed with jubilant toasts and heartfelt stories from beloved friends and family, weaving together a captivating tapestry of love and shared memories. Amid the lively festivities, I found moments for quiet reflection. As I soaked in the joyful conversations surrounding me, my thoughts wandered back to those long nights in Cambodia—the soft whispers of prayers and the steadfast hope that had carried me through my toughest times. It served as a powerful reminder of my journey and how love has an extraordinary way of connecting our past with the present in the most beautiful manner.

As the celebrations started to fade, Mary and I quietly made our way to a secluded porch, away from the bustling reception hall. Under a stunning blanket of stars and the gentle melodies of a Georgia night, we sat side by side, fingers clasped together. "This is our new beginning," Mary said, her tone steady and serene. I nodded, my heart swelling with gratitude. "Every memory, every challenge from Cambodia has burned like a sacred ember within me, lighting the way for what lies ahead," I responded, my emotions resonating in the tranquility of that moment.

The following day was Christmas. Our two families came together at Mary's home to share in the celebration of the occasion, both Christmas and our wedding. Gifts were shared, a small shower was given in Mary's honor, and a wonderful day was shared by all.

In the weeks that followed, we discovered refuge in a tranquil cabin nestled in the breathtaking North Georgia mountains—an idyllic getaway that Mary had thoughtfully designed for our honeymoon. Surrounded by towering pine trees and the gentle sounds of clear streams, our mornings were filled with the enjoyment of rich, aromatic local coffee on the cabin's delightful porch. As dusk settled in, we immersed ourselves in the vastness of the night sky, stargazing and dreaming of our future together. Each peaceful moment served as a poignant reminder that, while the past had shaped us, it also opened the door to new possibilities. Our journey together was intricately woven from the challenges we encountered and the aspirations we cherished, creating a beautiful tapestry of love and resilience.

As I stand on the brink of tomorrow, with Mary by my side and my heart brimming with gratitude and anticipation, I recognize the significance of our journey—every triumph and challenge, every word shared and those left unvoiced—has led us to this crucial moment. Our wedding day represents more than just a celebration of our love; it encapsulates the incredible strength of hope, the joy of shared laughter, and the steadfast commitment of two souls devoted to facing life's unpredictable adventure together.

Mary's visa and passport were in hand as we made our way to the Atlanta airport days later with several packed suitcases, all bound for a world of adventure in God-only-knows-where! We were both ready for the challenge.

Chapter Five

What the Future Holds

As we returned to Battambang after our wedding, I was deeply moved by the weight and promise that lingered in the air from the past few months. My six-month experience here had immersed me in the nuances of the language, with each hesitant phrase I learned revealing a richer understanding of the culture, intertwined in every shared smile and quiet prayer. Now, as I watched Mary step into this vibrant world for the first time, everything around us transformed—like rediscovering a cherished story, now illuminated by a language I could finally comprehend. The familiar sights took on fresh significance, filling me with an exhilarating sense of adventure waiting for us both.

As I stepped down from the weathered pickup in front of the Methodist Center, I glanced at Mary. The humid air embraced us with the heady scent of frangipani and the rich, earthy aroma of monsoon-drenched soil, feeling like an old friend. Her wide eyes took in the peaceful flow of life along the dusty streets. "Harold," she murmured, awe and admiration lacing her tone as we strolled by vibrant market stalls bursting with color, "I never realized a place could radiate such raw beauty and hold so much history." A wave of pride surged within me, mingling with gratitude for this land.

"This is Cambodia," I replied softly, my heart swelling with emotion. "Every corner here tells stories of spirit and hope, just waiting to be uncovered."

Brad and Charlie had already left for their mountain missions to create new churches and to work with the locals, so the Methodist Center was quiet, except for the welcoming embrace of Brother Rupert.

"Welcome to Paradise Mrs. Harold Brown!" exclaimed Brother Rupert. "We are so happy to have you in our beautiful country and have a home prepared for you both just around the corner." With that, Rupert carried us to our new home, and we settled in.

Mary found it unconscionable to have a gas burner for a stove instead of an actual stove! There was a modest double bed they would share with barely little space when the two slept side-by-side. It was a small dwelling, but they both vowed to make it home.

In the days that followed, Mary fully immersed herself in the lively pulse of local life. At a charming school decorated with vibrant children's artwork and chalk-drawn lessons, she began teaching English with an inspiring confidence that unveiled a new side of herself. I often found myself quietly standing in the doorway, captivated as she knelt beside the eager faces of her students. Her laughter—light and melodious—blended seamlessly with the joyful giggles that filled the room. A compassionate teacher approached Mary, her English hesitant yet heartfelt, and said, "You bring a new light to our school, ma'am." As I watched Mary absorb those words with true humility and happiness, I realized she was no longer just a visitor; she was becoming a vital part of this community, exuding warmth and a sense of belonging.

Mary would also work in the afternoons with her job at the center, documenting the various works that were in progress across the region, keeping books, and allocating funds for various ministries. She enjoyed her work and especially meeting the people each day.

As Mary fully committed herself to her role in the community, I devoted my time to my ministry at the Methodist Center. Each Sunday, I participated in heartfelt prayers with Pastor Chan and the congregation, administered communion, and had the privilege of baptizing several enthusiastic individuals. With my guitar in tow, I started to merge the well-loved melodies of English hymns with Khmer phrases—a daring and imaginative venture that quickly led to meaningful discussions. The community's warm smiles and encouraging nods conveyed so much, reminding me daily that love is a universal language that goes beyond words.

It didn't take long for personal happiness to beautifully intertwine with our shared mission. One tranquil evening, as twilight wrapped our guesthouse in a soft glow and the first stars began to sparkle in the deepening sky, Mary pulled me close on the back veranda. Her eyes, shimmering with the light of a lantern and the weight of unspoken emotions, fixed on mine.

"Harold Brown," she started, a slight quiver in her voice revealing both her vulnerability and hope, "I have something significant to tell you." In that delicate moment, embraced by the gentle chorus of nocturnal creatures, she shared the wonderful news: she was pregnant. The word lingered in the warm, humid air, sealing a promise that our small family was about to grow. I took her hand, overwhelmed by a rush of awe and tenderness.

"This is nothing short of a miracle," I murmured, each word infused with deep emotion. "Our journey together will be forever changed by the arrival of new life."

Seven months later, our lives were forever changed with the arrival of our son, Bradly Marion Brown. The memory of that day is etched in my heart: a gentle knock at the door heralded a moment I had longed for, accompanied by the comforting presence of Pastor Chan's wife, who had become a cherished friend during Mary's beautiful journey of anticipation. As I held that tiny, luminous life in my arms for the first time, an overwhelming wave of joy washed over me. Brad's birth was more than just a personal milestone; it echoed the lessons we learned in Battambang—the enduring strength, vibrant beauty, and indomitable spirit of a people who confront adversity with un-wavering courage and continue to sing their re-silient song.

As Brad matured, Mary's passion for storytelling blossomed. Her articles and photographs—vivid-ly portraying the essence of Cambodian life and offering deep insights into the vibrant local cul-ture—began appearing in esteemed publications, with National Geographic acknowledging her re-markable talent. Just when we thought life couldn't become more beautiful, it had another delightful surprise: only a year after Brad's arrival, Mary found out she was expecting again.

When the news broke, our home was filled with an almost sacred joy. Soon, we welcomed a healthy baby girl, Penelope Christian Brown, affectionately known as "Penny." Each laugh, every whispered promise, and all the joyful exchanges shared as we held our children deepened our bond—not only with each other but also with this extraordinary land we call home. These moments of love and discovery continue to weave our narrative together, enriching our lives in ways that words can scarcely capture.

Pastor Chan's wife, Hounee, cared for our two children while Mary and I worked each day and became an indispensable help in our time of need. She would even teach them Khmer words that would help them both in the future. She helped us through many childhood illnesses with local remedies, for which we were most thankful.

Sopheak followed me now everywhere I went. He had learned English exceptionally well and I too, had learned Khmer, so our cooperation together was tangible. He was now ready to begin teaching English to the students at the local Methodist school and I was most proud of him.

As our family grew, so did the deepening commitment to our mission. Merely two years after Penny came on board, we were surprised with a thrilling message from our home office—a letter overflowing with promise. It was an invitation to spearhead our mission in Tarangambadi, India, an opportunity that would change our lives forever.

I can still feel the rush of adrenaline as I read the letter, my heart pounding with the thrill of sharing this groundbreaking news with Mary. "We have just a month to get ready," I said, my voice trembling with a blend of eagerness and excitement.

Mary's eyes shone with steadfast resolve as she squeezed my hand firmly. "Let's seize this opportunity," she replied without hesitation.

In that moment, the road ahead revealed itself—brimming with potential and shimmering with the excitement of fresh starts. We teetered on the edge of an incredible journey, prepared to embrace the future and create a meaningful change.

Before we departed, we hosted a profoundly meaningful farewell gathering in Battambang—a celebration honoring the deep connections we had created during these transformative months. Lanterns lit up the trees, casting a warm glow as twilight surrounded us, while the aroma of local dishes filled the air, harmonizing with the gentle rhythm of rain tapping on the dusty ground. Friends, neighbors, and

cherished members of our congregation united, creating a touching atmosphere as they said a bittersweet
yet hopeful goodbye. I can still picture Sopheak, my
devoted protégé, standing beside me, expressing his
heartfelt thoughts in a way that beautifully encapsulated the essence of our shared journey.

"Harold," he said, "your steadfast support has given
me the confidence to believe in myself and my dreams.
I vow to honor your trust in me and strive to make you
proud, no matter where life's path takes us."

His voice, infused with a quivering resolve and a
sparkle in his eyes, struck a chord with the essence
of our community. Mary, her voice brimming with
genuine gratitude, mirrored his feelings: "Although we
may be going our separate ways, this is not the conclusion. The bonds we've created here are enduring and
will always stay in our hearts, a tribute to our time in
Battambang."

That evening, as the music floated through the
warm air—my guitar strumming a tender, bittersweet
tune that harmonized perfectly with the laughter and
joyful voices of children—we came together to bid our

farewells. Every heartfelt handshake and tearful embrace served as a poignant reminder of the profound
impression Cambodia had made on our souls. It was a
farewell brimming with emotion, with each moment
standing as a tribute to the unforgettable journey we
experienced and the connections we forged in this enchanting land.

With our hearts overflowing with love and treasured
memories, we climbed aboard our awaiting transport,
ready to begin the next chapter of our adventure in
India. As the familiar sights of Cambodia gradually
faded from view, I glanced at Mary, Brad, and little
Penny, fully realizing how transformative our time in
Battambang had been—filled with growth, miracles,
and deep connections. This remarkable journey was
sure to light the way for our new life in Tarangambadi,
India, enhancing our experiences and enriching our
lives in ways we could hardly fathom.

In that instant, my spirit flared with exhilarating
anticipation and profound gratitude. Each farewell
signified not just an ending, but the emergence of a
new beginning; every tear shed was a reminder that
love would persist, overcoming any distance. As we set

forth on our next journey, I clung to the essence of Battambang—its joy, its invaluable teachings, its people, and its resolute spirit. By my side was the unyielding connection of a family bound by hope, prepared to face the future together.

CHAPTER SIX

India: A Journey of Purpose

Upon our arrival in Tarangambadi, India, we were instantly enveloped by a stunning blend of color, sound, and fragrance that awakened our senses. The city pulsated with energy: the distant chime of temple bells echoed through the labyrinthine streets, vendors welcomed us with their harmonious calls, and the alluring scent of incense mingled beautifully with the rich aromas of exotic spices. This enchanting destination felt worlds away from the tranquil scenery of Cambodia, beckoning us to immerse ourselves fully in its vibrant tapestry of life.

Mary's eyes glimmered with enthusiasm as we stepped into this energetic new realm. Strolling through the bustling market streets, she absorbed every detail, exclaiming, "Harold, this place is alive—it's infused with passion and history!"

I nodded, my thoughts wandering to the prayers and minor victories from my last mission. "This," I said softly, "is India—a place where each day unravels like a vibrant tapestry of resilience and hope."

As always, the children reveled in the exhilaration of their unfamiliar environment with limitless enthusiasm. Brad's laughter resonated throughout the lively market, his spirit shining brightly as he darted effortlessly among the colorful stalls. Little Penny burst with joy, squealing in delight at the sight of the vibrant kites soaring gracefully in the sky above. Their infectious energy served as a beautiful reminder that every fresh start is infused with the thrill of exploration, even amidst uncertainty. In their eyes, what might seem like danger turned into an exciting adventure, igniting a spark of wonder that inspired those around them.

That promise crystallized sharply one radiant afternoon as we delved into the vibrant core of the market—a lively labyrinth of narrow streets pulsing with activity. While Mary animatedly conversed with a cheerful spice vendor, a chilling realization hit me:

Brad was no longer by my side. Panic gripped my chest as I shouted his name, my voice barely cutting through the lively din of the marketplace. My heart raced in my ears when I caught sight of his small, determined figure veering perilously close to an oncoming rickshaw. "Brad! Stop!" I cried out, the urgency in my tone swallowed by the surrounding clamor.

In that agonizing moment, time seemed to elongate, the rickshaw's blaring horn blending with the frantic pounding of my heart. I lunged forward, seizing his arm just before he stepped into harm's way. As I pulled him back, a wave of relief washed over me, intertwined with a profound, wrenching fear. It became painfully evident that every heartbeat, every fleeting moment, is a treasured gift that can disappear in an instant.

As we sat in our modest accommodation, savoring our steaming cups of spiced tea, Mary and I slipped into a reflective silence, each of us immersed in our thoughts about the day's distressing events. "Today, my angel teetered too close to danger," I murmured, my voice laden with both regret and profound gratitude. "We were lucky to step in just when we did—it's a stark reminder of how precious every moment really is."

After that distressing scare, our lives took a surprising turn that we hadn't foreseen. With the steadfast support of our local community, we decided to enroll Brad and Penny in a nearby school—a delightful institution that embraced children from diverse backgrounds each morning. This school became a vibrant reflection of Indian life; classrooms buzzed with a harmonious blend of languages, blackboards brimmed with lessons in mathematics and local history, and the cheerful laughter of children echoed, effortlessly bridging cultural gaps. It was evident that this nurturing environment was more than just a place of learning; it was a community where connections were nurtured, understanding blossomed, and futures were illuminated.

I distinctly remember the first morning I noticed Brad in class. He sat in his designated spot within the arranged rows, his eyes glimmering with a mix of curiosity and determination as the teacher guided us through an English lesson. Impressively, he was swiftly acquiring this new language, effortlessly blending lighthearted conversation with serious practice. What stood out to me the most was the maturity he exhibited; his youthful energy harmonized with a new-found sense of responsibility. I observed him listening intently, asking thoughtful questions, and even helping a younger classmate struggling with a difficult word. In that moment, it became evident to me: Brad was not just playing in the lively streets—he was maturing, consciously absorbing the knowledge of a world that extended far beyond our immediate tasks. His development served as a powerful reminder of the transformative influence of learning and the potential that lies ahead.

Even at such an early age, Penny represented transformation in her delightful way. In the schoolyard, her laughter blended with her friends' as they uncovered the joys of writing letters and solving simple puzzles. Her eyes shone with the thrill of new knowledge, hinting at a bright future awaiting her. I was continually amazed at how quickly the children were growing in this lively environment; each school day evolved into more than just academics—it became a deep lesson in grasping the fragile essence of life and a poignant reminder to cherish every precious moment.

At school, teachers adeptly integrated standard academics with essential lessons in character and community values. Before long, Brad and Penny began to seamlessly merge English with the local dialect, creating a rich tapestry of cultures that embodied the bright potential of their future. The daily bell signaling the start of classes was not just a cue for learning but a reminder of the lively spirit of life in Tarangambadi. Each moment transformed into a cherished building block in the development of their identities, molding them into self-assured individuals prepared to take on the world.

As I observed the incredible growth of the children, my dedication to the community deepened more than ever. I spent countless hours at the local gathering place, collaborating with fellow missionaries and local leaders to identify the best ways to nurture the spirit of our shared mission. During this journey, I began to merge English hymns with elements of Hindi and Tamil, creating melodies that, though initially a bit awkward, soon transformed into a strong symbol of our unity across cultures and generations. These songs not only resonated within our diverse community but also strengthened our connections, capturing the essence of our collective purpose. I played the guitar while another missionary played the sitar. It was an interesting but compelling sound.

On a bright afternoon, as I sat comfortably on a solid stone bench shaded by the sprawling branches of old mango trees, I watched a vibrant scene come to life in the school courtyard. A spirited group of children was caught up in a joyful game of tag, with Brad's laughter echoing like a sweet symbol of innocence amidst the fun. Their cheerful shouts blended seamlessly with the soft murmur of prayers and the distant chime of temple bells, serving as a touching reminder of the fragile beauty of life.

Following the earlier scare, my viewpoint underwent a significant transformation. I started to see their education not just as a way to gain knowledge but as an essential stronghold protecting their futures. I realized that even in a world filled with unpredictability and dangers, the foundations of hope and learning remained steadfast. This insight sparked a deep understanding: by valuing education, these children transcended the role of mere students; they became the builders of their own destinies, embodying resilience in an uncertain landscape.

As the months rolled by, our mission in Tarangambadi flourished with untiring resolve. Each day unfolded new adventures, interwoven with experiences that brought joy, imparted deep lessons, and sometimes introduced heartache—each moment serving as a vivid reflection of life's vibrant tapestry. Meanwhile, Mary dedicated herself to capturing the essence of India's rich and diverse culture through her writing. Our children thrived in this nurturing atmosphere, their youthful energy blossoming magnificently as they absorbed the invaluable wisdom that accompanies growing up. Each day, we observed their transformations, a poignant reminder of the incredible journey we were all sharing together.

After a couple of years in Tarangambadi, we received a two-month furlough to return home to Georgia. We were all ecstatic and looked forward to reuniting with our families. While there we had serious conversations with our parents about the children and their need for more structured learning. While Mary and I disagreed with our parents, we came to realize that they were perhaps right. The children could both use a more structured environment in the coming years.

My mother took it upon herself to invite the children to come live with her and my father upon our next furlough home in two years. Since both families were only a block apart, they both agreed to share in the caring for the children while we expanded our missions in India. This opened many doors for us although we would miss our children.

We returned to India with the children and began preparing them for their return to Georgia in two years while on furlough. They were both excited about new adventures and welcomed the change.

One crisp morning, nearly two years later, a letter from our headquarters arrived, sparking a sense of excitement and endless possibilities. It was an invitation to expand our mission deep into the heart of India, marking yet another significant chapter in our journey. As Mary and I sat across from one another at the breakfast table, our eyes locked in silent understanding, while the children busied themselves with their morning routines in the background.

"A new beginning is on the horizon," Mary murmured, her voice steady and filled with determination.

We both recognized that this was more than just an opportunity; it represented the promise of trans-formative change, not just for us but for those we were meant to serve. We also knew that we would have to take that furlough home to situate the children with our parents before taking the new mission, which we did.

Amid challenges, we uncovered our resilience in the rhythm of school bells and the boundless opportunities education offers. Each hurdle became a crucial steppingstone toward a more promising future. Observing Brad and Penny blossom in confidence each day reassured me that the lessons they learned within those classroom walls would serve as guiding lights back in Georgia, illuminating our path as we embark on this significant journey together without the children.

After a one-month furlough home, we returned to India without the children. Our hearts were breaking but we tried not to let it show. God had called us to this new mission which we would embrace wholehearted-ly. The call of God usually involves sacrifices, but we both had signed up for just such a situation. We knew that our children were in good hands.

Chapter Seven

Back to India

Following the tumult of emotions, we encountered during our initial years of service in Tarangambadi and the heartbreaking release of our children back in Georgia, life has slowly found a comforting cadence. The hardships we faced, coupled with the traumatic event that nearly took Brad from us, have only deepened our connection as a family. Each day, as Mary and I step into our roles, we aren't merely serving as missionaries in India; we are nurturing our India family, firmly rooted in love, resilience, and purpose. Together, we are devoted to making an impact, and with each shared experience, our bond and determination only strengthen.

The early mornings here overflow with unspoken potential. As dawn's first light breaks, I awaken before the sun, surrounded by the soft hum of the city awakening. The distant tolling of temple bells mingles with the gentle chatter of vendors setting up their stalls, while I inhale the cool, fragrant air, rich with the enchanting scents of jasmine and spice. In these tranquil moments, I find solace on our little veranda, guitar in hand, where reflection becomes a cherished ritual. Each note I play resonates with the gratitude I carry for the vibrant tapestry of experiences that have shaped our journey here—every smile shared with locals, every lesson learned, and each sacred prayer whispered beneath the vast Indian sky. In this beautiful symphony of life, I am reminded that every sunrise heralds the chance for new beginnings and deeper connections.

My mission work has transformed into an active partnership with local pastors and community leaders at a lively community center brimming with energy. Under the expansive canopy of ancient mango trees, we hold inspiring council meetings that extend into the afternoon, nurturing creativity and vision. Together, we develop outreach programs that harmoniously integrate our fundamental Christian values with vibrant indigenous traditions, promoting unity and respect.

As I endeavor to blend English hymns with phrases from Hindi and Tamil, what started as a tentative effort has blossomed into a heartfelt expression that truly connects with the community. Every time I witness a local elder smile at one of my adapted verses, I am deeply affirmed in my conviction that our ministry in India goes beyond simple spirituality; it is deeply grounded in our shared humanity. This endeavor is not solely focused on faith; it is about creating cultural bridges and fostering connections that enhance both our spiritual journeys and the community we serve.

Mary is our steadfast beacon of grace and storytelling talent. With her ever-present notebook and an empathetic gaze, she masterfully captures the vibrant tapestry of life that unfolds around us each day. Whether she's immersed in the bustling atmosphere of a local school courtyard—where children joyfully share their lessons in a charming mix of English and their native language—or partaking in a delightful tea gathering at a neighbor's home, Mary's writing reflects a profound understanding of India's essence. Her narratives, rich with vivid imagery and deep reflection, illuminate a land that embodies both resilience and gentleness, echoing sentiments that resonate with all who encounter her work. Mary's gift for transforming these experiences into engaging stories not only enhances our understanding but also invites us to appreciate the beauty and intricacy of life in India through her perspective.

The children have truly thrived in their new surroundings. Brad, full of youthful vigor, is making impressive progress as he adapts to the structure of school life in Georgia. Penny is now in the first grade and doing very well, according to our parents. We call them once a week to check in and hear their sweet voices. We look forward to our next two-year furlough to spend a couple of months with them. We have a whirlwind vacation to several states with them during that time.

As the days grow longer and our workloads intensify, we are constantly reminded of the challenges we face and the preciousness of every moment. I can still vividly recall that fateful afternoon at the market—a day that fundamentally shifted our perspective and taught us a profound lesson: the fragility of life warrants our deepest gratitude. This truth resonates with me every day, especially when I witness Brad's steadfast determination or the awe in Penny's eyes. Amidst the vibrant chaos of India, it serves as a resonant reminder that every heartbeat is a gem. Let us cherish our existence with the appreciation it rightfully deserves.

As dusk settles over our lively community center, I frequently find myself engaged in poignant conversations with fellow missionaries and cherished local pastors. We go beyond mere discussions of ministry planning or future initiatives; we delve into the profound interplay between tradition and transformation.

One unforgettable night, under a sky blanketed in stars, a respected elder voiced a compelling thought: "Harold, your words and melodies resonate deeply with us. They guide us toward revitalizing our age-old traditions." In that moment, it became evident that our mission extends far beyond service—it's about intertwining our shared humanity, personal narratives, and faith into a rich tapestry that brings us together, bridging divides and fostering connections. Let's embark on this transformative journey, igniting hope and inspiring change within our community and beyond.

In these heartfelt moments of collective reflection—whether gathered around a simple meal rich in
local flavors or enveloped in the tranquility of com-
munal prayer—I observe the dynamic growth of our
ministry in India. Our work transcends mere commitment; it stands as a vibrant testament to our extraordinary ability to transform challenges into significant opportunities for renewal. It is through the warm
exchange of smiles, the sparks of hope ignited in our
meaningful conversations, and the enlightening experiences in our lively classrooms that the true essence
of our mission is revealed. Together, we are not just
making an impact; we are nurturing a transformative
movement that inspires and uplifts communities.

As the morning sunlight gradually envelops the
courtyard in a warm embrace, I am overwhelmed with
gratitude while I take in the sight of my dear wife,
Mary, gathered around me, her presence igniting a
profound sense of purpose within. With Mary's empowering words resonating in my heart, our mission
in India evolves from a noble pursuit into the very
heart of our existence. It becomes a rich narrative that
highlights the beauty of service, the strength of com-

munity, and the untiring power of love. Together, we aren't merely chasing a dream; we are embarking on a journey that embodies hope and inspiration for both ourselves and those we strive to uplift.

As twilight settled over the tranquil evening in Tarangambadi, I sat on the veranda with Mary, the familiar sounds of our community center gently fading into the distance. Our hearts overflowed with gratitude, and we walked with conviction—our experience in India had deeply enriched our faith and transformed our lives in ways we had never imagined. However, on that magical evening, as a soft breeze swept through, carrying the distant chime of temple bells, a sudden knock at the door interrupted our peaceful moment, calling us toward an unexpected event of immense importance.

Bathed in the soft glow of a lantern, a messenger emerged—a reliable envoy from the Indian Bishop, bringing news that stirred a blend of excitement and anxiety within me. With a sense of quiet urgency, he shared that, after careful reflection, the church leadership had recognized the growth and resilience of our ministry, the unbreakable ties of our family, and the enduring impact we've made in this land. Consequently, we have been entrusted with a remarkable new mission: to begin a journey in Suriname, a far-off paradise surrounded by lush rainforests and vibrant indigenous cultures. This opportunity represents not just a relocation; it is a chance to expand our influence and nurture meaningful relationships in a place abundant with potential for our shared passion and purpose.

Mary and I exchanged a meaningful glance, one that captured the bittersweet nature of farewell alongside the thrilling promise of a fresh start. Though it was difficult to contemplate leaving behind the beloved community we had come to cherish, we understood that our journey of service was a firm commitment, urging us onward. With a blend of nervousness and eager excitement, we embraced this divine calling, prepared to uncover the opportunities that lay ahead.

As I closed my eyes that night, the lingering resonance of that pivotal message mingled with the soft whispers of the Indian evening, signaling not an end, but the beginning of an extraordinary journey. It called me to step beyond the known boundaries of

Tarangambadi and welcome the endless opportunities that awaited us in Suriname.

Being a missionary is about humility and "going where sent." We embrace this change with much anticipation and a bit of anxiety. We will be embracing a rainforest in South America and do not know what to expect.

With our furlough coming between moves, we packed up all of our belongings and traveled home to Georgia for our time with the children and family.

CHAPTER EIGHT

Suriname

I vividly remember the day we departed from India, as if it were indelibly marked in my mind. That cool evening, when the messenger's words struck a chord within us, set in motion our remarkable adventure. After a brief visit back to Georgia, we soon found ourselves on a riverboat, navigating the lush heart of Suriname—a stunning land where the river wound through a vibrant green canopy like an essential lifeline. It was a captivating world that called to us with its promise of exploration and excitement. Each leaf glimmered with morning dew, and the gentle rustle of the ancient trees shared the secrets of our forebears. The air was thick with the enchanting scents of wild orchids and fertile soil, wrapping us in an atmosphere brimming with potential. This was more than a mere journey; it was the awakening of our souls in a land rich with mystery and charm.

We were thankful that the children were not with us at this point. There were many dangers along the river and in the remote village where we were heading. We were told to keep our eyes open and to be aware of certain dangers while in-country.

Entering the captivating village of Kondoribo was truly a transformative journey. Nestled in a secluded part of the world, this indigenous community stands resilient amidst the vibrant tapestry of a tropical rainforest, exuding a sense of warmth and intrigue. Upon our arrival, we were greeted with cautious yet genuine smiles, while the resonant beat of ceremonial drums filled the air, producing a rhythm that felt both timeless and vibrant.

The villagers possessed an extraordinary aura, embodying a serene dignity that conveyed much more than words could express. Adorned in traditional attire bursting with vivid hues and detailed designs, their clothing told stories that had been passed down

through countless generations, reflecting their profound bond with the land.

An elder, with a face marked by the wisdom of ages,
grasped my hand in a gesture that transcended language. "Welcome, my friend," he softly intoned, his
voice rich with respect. "Our ancestors have eagerly
anticipated your coming."

In that significant moment, it seemed as if the soul
of the forest fused with our own, forging a connection
that was at once humbling and thrilling. This location
transcended mere geography; it represented a sacred
link to a lineage that reached back through the ages,
inviting us to deeply engage with the vibrant tapestry
of their heritage.

In Suriname, our mission went beyond simple outreach; it was a genuine effort to serve as a bridge—a
crucial link between our cherished faith and the
deep-rooted traditions of the indigenous communities. Collaborating with local leaders and committed missionaries, Mary and I enthusiastically devel-
oped community outreach initiatives centered around
health education, literacy, and sustainable develop-

ment, always with a deep respect for and appreciation of the native way of life. Mary continued draft-
ing new articles and taking photos that were amazing.

We dived deep into the rich culture, attentively absorbing the enthralling tales handed down through
the ages regarding their rituals and legends, while
gaining a deeper understanding of their profound
connection with nature. In this reciprocal dialogue, I
recounted my own transformative experiences, echoing the powerful truth that each life and tradition is
an essential thread in the beautiful tapestry of God's
creation. Together, we sought to foster a collective
dedication to uplift and empower, ensuring that the
vibrancy of their heritage thrives alongside our faith.

Mary's love for storytelling, which had begun to
blossom during our time in India, reached extraordinary heights in Kondoribo. With her ever-present
notebook in hand, she wandered along the shaded paths and immersed herself in local tea gatherings, highlighting a graceful curiosity that enchanted
everyone she encountered.

In those intimate moments tucked beneath the dense foliage, she collected stories of healing herbs, ancient rituals, and the remarkable resilience of the community. Her articles, vibrant with detailed descriptions and deep personal insights, swiftly garnered national attention. One standout piece featured in a renowned magazine artfully highlighted the delicate balance between tradition and the modern challenges confronting Kondoribo, earning her critical acclaim and invitations to speak at various cultural events. Her writing, as radiant as sunlight streaming through the leaves, not only enlightened readers but also inspired a ripple of enthusiasm that resonated well beyond our village.

Amidst the vibrant and lush tapestry of existence, our journey unfolded alongside its share of daunting challenges. One sweltering afternoon, as dark clouds gathered over the rainforest, Mary's health took a grave turn. What began as a mild fever quickly escalated into a serious respiratory infection. I can still recall the chilling fear that gripped me as Mary was rushed to the small, community-operated clinic—a humble establishment built by the resilient hands of the people of Kondoribo. There, local doctors combined traditional remedies with modern medical practices, dedicating themselves to a night of intense effort to stabilize her condition. Throughout those agonizing hours, Mary clutched my hand tightly, our silent prayers interweaving in a bond of steadfast support.

As the first light of dawn arrived and Mary's fever finally began to subside, a deep sense of gratitude enveloped us, intertwined with the remnants of lingering fear. This harrowing experience, while frightening at the time, instilled a steadfast determination in us. It became the catalyst for one of Mary's most compelling articles—a heartfelt plea for improved healthcare resources in our isolated communities. Her powerful words struck a chord, resonating profoundly with both readers and policymakers, sparking an essential dialogue about the healthcare inequities that frequently impact those on the fringes of society.

In the tranquil stillness of dawn, as the sky shifted from deep indigo to brilliant gold, I found myself perched on the wooden steps of our modest home, surrounded by the soothing melodies of the rainforest. In those reflective moments, I pondered how the formidable voice of Kondoribo embodies the complex interplay between our cultural heritage and modern progress. It serves as a poignant reminder that our mission here goes beyond simply confronting immediate challenges; we are also called to sow the seeds for a future filled with healing and harmony. The same lifeblood that accompanied us from the bustling streets of India to this magical retreat now flows through our veins, igniting within us a renewed strength, born from both our trials and triumphs. Together, we are not merely witnessing transformation; we are actively contributing to it.

Evenings in Kondoribo were draped in a serene, almost magical quietude. Under the shimmering starlit sky, the village sprang to life around flickering flames as neighbors gathered to share not just food but a rich tapestry of stories and laughter that seamlessly blended with nature's nighttime symphony.

Mary possessed a remarkable talent for capturing these community moments, documenting each heartfelt conversation and the wisdom of the elders with an intensity that resonated well beyond her written words. As we savored aromatic cups of spiced herbal tea, local storytellers spun enchanting narratives of forest spirits and ancient guardians, making it feel as though those timeless protectors were walking beside us. In those treasured moments, it became evident to me that our purpose here extended beyond mere physical labor; it was a profound exchange of souls, an extraordinary journey into the very heart of existence.

As I stand beneath a stunningly vast sky, filled with countless stars and surrounded by the vibrant energy of the rainforest at my feet, I feel the immense weight and extraordinary potential of destiny. Suriname beckons us to rise above our limitations and embrace a powerful blend of faith, culture, and nature—a true beacon of hope for the future. Each sunrise that paints the horizon with its vivid colors serves as a poignant reminder that the seeds we sow in these ancient lands and in our hearts will blossom into deep healing for generations ahead. In this rich amalgamation of elements, we uncover the possibilities for transformative change, illuminating the path toward a brighter tomorrow.

As I embark on this new and uncharted chapter, I carry with me an unwavering belief that our journey will flow like the majestic rivers of Suriname, leading us to a future filled with purpose, unity, and the deep beauty of our shared humanity. Inspired by Mary's award-winning articles that have resonated with so many and driven by the resilience our family has built through challenges, our mission in Suriname is set to be both transformative and unforgettable. It serves as a powerful reminder of the lasting strength found in service, love, and unwavering hope.

Chapter Nine

The Call to Guyana

As Mary and I stood before the stunning landscape of Kondoribo, we faced a significant turning point. Our children—Brad, who was about to start his college adventure, and Penny, mere weeks from graduating with dreams of becoming a nurse—needed their parents to come home and counsel them in their life choices.

We asked for and were granted a two-month furlough to return to Georgia and counsel with our children. Our trip would allow us time to help them with college applications and student loans and to discuss exactly what plans they were choosing. Our parents had been most helpful in this respect, so our jobs were much easier than we had thought. We had two wonderful months with our parents and the children but knew that we were destined to return after our furlough ended.

After our return to Kondoribo, we worked tirelessly in helping the locals for two more years before the call came once again for us to move to a new ministry. We were contacted by the missions board to move to a wonderful opportunity next door in Guyana.

Mary and I were irresistibly drawn to this higher calling. Our fate lay in Moraikobal, a hidden village within the rainforest of Guyana, untouched by any missionary efforts until now.

After bidding emotional goodbyes in Kondoribo, we gathered our few possessions and embarked on a journey that promised to be our most challenging to date. This was more than merely traveling; it was a mission to bring hope and create a positive change in a community that had never before felt our presence.

Our adventure began with a thrilling and perilous boat ride along the winding Essequibo River, where shadowy waters snake beneath an endless canopy, hinting at an untamed world beyond. Just halfway through our journey, our unassuming craft encountered an unforeseen dilemma, running aground on a shifting sandbar. For three agonizing hours, Mary and I endured a heavy silence, the rising tide looming ominously, as if poised to imprison us in this remote wilderness for eternity. Meanwhile, the eerie cries of howler monkeys reverberated through the air, and brilliant birds flitted against a lush emerald backdrop, each sound and sight a captivating reminder of nature's wild beauty—and its unpredictable dangers.

After successfully liberating our vessel from the grip of the sandbar, we forged ahead, unaware of the remarkable changes that awaited us onshore. As nightfall painted the horizon and we neared Moraikobal, the lush jungle revealed its dual nature—both stunningly beautiful and incredibly treacherous. Upon reaching the village, we encountered the locals, their wary yet warm smiles conveying an understanding of the forest's wild power.

With their help, we unloaded our provisions and soon found ourselves atop a creaky, lantern-lit wagon, journeying to our new home. It stood there—a cozy thatched-roof hut on the edge of Moraikobal, a humble sanctuary that promised fresh beginnings in a land teeming with mystery and awe.

The first nights felt like a true ordeal. The thick, humid air within the hut buzzed with the vibrant energy of the jungle, making it clear that we were not alone. As darkness fell, massive tarantulas—glimmering with beads of moisture and moving with astonishing speed—began to emerge from the walls and floor. They scuttled quietly in the shadows, a constant reminder that danger was lurking just out of sight in this untamed paradise. I remembered the villagers' urgent warnings about keeping our camp tidy and building barriers to ward off these nighttime visitors. With every careful adjustment we made, we adapted to our new reality, turning fear into survival.

One of the most terrifying experiences of my life unfolded during a dawn mission to fetch water from a nearby stream. As I crouched by the water's edge, the peaceful atmosphere was suddenly disrupted by a foreboding rustle among the reeds. My heart raced as I turned to see a massive anaconda, its body mostly submerged, ready to strike. Its slow, deliberate movements sent a surge of adrenaline through me, and for a moment, I was frozen in fear. Just as swiftly as it had emerged, the serpent disappeared into the murky water, leaving me breathless. In that chilling moment, I grasped a profound truth: in this wild, untamed realm, the line between beauty and peril is as fragile and temporary as a single dewdrop hanging onto a leaf.

Each day in Moraikobal presented a profound lesson in awareness and appreciation. As the sun rose, the jungle morphed into an enchanting tapestry of life and color. Tropical birds flitted by, displaying their vibrant hues, while the leaves underfoot shared their quiet secrets, and golden beams of sunlight streamed through the dense canopy above. Local villagers, stewards of ancient forest knowledge, led Mary and me through its complexities. They taught us which paths were safe and shared their invaluable expertise on creating natural remedies for bothersome insect bites. We also learned powerful chants to seek protection as night fell. Over time, we cultivated a deep trust in the mesmerizing rhythm of this wild landscape, allowing its magic to resonate within our hearts.

Amid the unyielding challenges, a striking beauty unfolded. In those tranquil moments just before dawn, I would settle onto the wooden steps of our modest hut, enveloped by the enchanting lullabies of the rainforest. The haunting calls of nighttime creatures melded with the gentle flow of the river, creating a mesmerizing symphony that stirred both trepidation and inspiration. Often, Mary would join me in this reflective hour, and together we contemplated our journey. While our children were lovingly looked after back home, we remained resolute in our mission, unshaken by the shadows of fear that occasionally crept in. Our spirits, honed by adversity, resonated with unwavering hope that fueled our determination.

"Harold Brown, I remember telling you once that I would go wherever you went. Now look at me, here in this jungle paradise, and loving every minute of it," Mary exclaimed with grace.

"I appreciate you so much, Mary," I replied. "You have been a godsend to me and the many missions we have undertaken. Who knows where it will end?"

That evening, surrounded by the gentle flicker of candlelight, Mary and I huddled together, contemplating the day's profound insights. The eerie call of an unseen predator resonated in the shadows, and the unsettling scurry of tarantulas by the door heightened our senses. Then, there was the chilling encounter with the anaconda—a stark reminder that in the jungle, every heartbeat is not merely a moment to survive but a vital lesson in resilience. We made a heartfelt promise to carry these lessons into our future pursuits, welcoming each challenge as a chance to fortify our resolve and deepen our unwavering faith. Together, we recognized that the obstacles we encounter only serve to sharpen our determination and illuminate our path ahead.

While in Guyana, Mary and I taught classes underneath a thatched pavilion each day and talked to the children about Christ. On one occasion, I was delighted to baptize thirty-eight youth in the Essequibo River! It was a glorious occasion and would remain in my memory for the rest of my life.

Back home, Mary's articles and photography gleaned numerous awards, and her pay helped our ministries here in Guyana. Everything was for the grace of God.

As the first rays of dawn broke over the horizon, casting a soft golden light on the lush greens of Moraikobal, I couldn't help but recognize a profound realization. Our expedition through Guyana was fraught with danger and unpredictability, yet it was in facing these formidable challenges that the essence of hope and resilience shone through most clearly. Deep within the uncharted rainforest, where nature continuously pushed us to our limits, Mary and I uncovered the true strength of adaptability. We learned to protect our small haven and appreciate every precious moment of life. It was through these hardships that we utterly understood the significance of perseverance and gratitude, forming an unbreakable connection with the wild that would forever shape our souls.

After three more years in Guyana, we received our next furlough home to Georgia. We were more than ready to see our children and parents.

Chapter Ten

Georgia On Our Mind

The airplane touched down on Georgia soil with a reassuring thud, a sound that swiftly dispelled the haunting memories of the wild Guyanese jungles. After three years of navigating treacherous rivers, enduring unsettling nights filled with the rustling of tarantulas, and encountering the silent presence of elusive anacondas in Moraikobal, Mary and I had finally returned home. We inhaled the fragrant air infused with magnolia and were welcomed by warm, familiar voices, relishing the comfort of our authentic sanctuary.

This six-week furlough came at a crucial time in Brad's life—during the spring break of his sophomore year. It represented a key shift from the carefree curiosity of childhood to the deeper passions of young adulthood. I can still picture our warm conversations in the comforting embrace of our family kitchen, where he eagerly recounted tales of his recent college debates and community initiatives. His eyes sparkled with the passionate belief that he had the power to make a real difference in the world. Despite the challenges he encountered while navigating the rich cultures of far-off places, he returned home with a newfound maturity that strengthened his resolve, while his steadfast spirit continued to inspire those around him. Georgia Tech was tough, but Brad was even tougher!

Penny has truly thrived through the trials and triumphs of our missionary work. Now a high school graduate, she has embarked on an exciting journey at South University in Savannah, eagerly beginning her first year in nursing—a field that perfectly aligns with her inherent compassion. Each late-night study session and hands-on experience during her clinical rotations have only strengthened her confidence. Over our morning coffees at the local diner, she shares her experiences with infectious enthusiasm, vividly describing hospital corridors alive with a dynamic mix of urgency and hope. In those moments, Penny bridges the stark realities of illness with the profound potential of compassionate care, embodying what it truly means to be a healer.

Mary, our family's devoted chronicler, found a fresh spark of inspiration in the beloved corners of Georgia. As she wandered through the historic streets of our hometown, discovering charming cafés and tucked-away bookstores, she gathered a wealth of memories that would soon evolve into a captivating series of reflective articles. In one particularly moving piece, she crafted a striking analogy between the quiet strength of Southern communities and the wild, untamed spirit we had encountered in the jungles of Guyana. Her words, rich with warmth and deep insight, beautifully conveyed a universal truth: regardless of where our adventures led us, home would forever be our sanctuary, a place where we could truly express our authentic selves.

Our time at home unfolded with a gentle rhythm, shaped by the warmth of family and cherished traditions. Sundays brought us together in worship, where the bond of community filled the church. We shared meals on our wraparound porches, where laughter and stories danced in the soft summer breeze. Countless evenings were spent in spontaneous conversations beneath the expansive, starry Georgia sky, each moment steeped in connection and nostalgia. Long drives along winding country roads, bordered by majestic oaks and fragrant magnolias, provided a peaceful retreat that renewed our spirits. These treasured experiences were more than mere moments of joy; they were lasting reminders of our heritage—a legacy that shaped us, even as the world beyond awakened our hearts to adventure and possibility. In the embrace of home, we discovered our anchor, a comforting reminder of who we are and where we truly belong.

Although our furlough brought joy, it was interwoven with a bittersweet sense of longing. Every warm laugh and nostalgic trip to cherished childhood spots carried with it the faint ache of separation from the people we had served in Guyana and from a mission that had transformed us. As I sat on the familiar front porch of our home in Webster, gently strumming my guitar, I couldn't help but ponder how the wild unpredictability of anacondas and tarantulas had been replaced by the steady, comforting rhythm of Southern life. It served as a poignant reminder of how deeply our experiences had influenced us, leaving a lasting impression on our hearts.

In these serene moments of contemplation, I envisioned a bright future for us. Our children would flourish, drawing from the rich experiences of two contrasting worlds—one exhilarating yet often intimidating, the other a steady haven infused with the warmth of home—embodying the resilience that defines the human spirit.

Mary's articles, gaining traction and inviting opportunities to speak at regional conferences, highlighted the intricate fusion of far-off adventures and our beloved Southern heritage. As we embraced each other tightly during heartfelt farewells with family, we recognized that this interlude was not just a pause, but an essential renewal—an opportunity to recharge our strength and clarity before the next call to move forward.

As our time in Georgia ended, we experienced a profound sense of fulfillment intertwined with a fresh wave of hope. This break had revitalized our spirits and rekindled our connection to our roots. With Brad embracing a renewed sense of purpose and Penny's steadfast dedication to her nursing career, Mary and I were prepared to face the future. We felt empowered by the invaluable lessons we'd learned both at home and abroad, confident that these insights would illuminate the next chapter of our journey.

Chapter Eleven

Return to Guyana

Following our revitalizing retreat in Georgia, I experienced a deep awakening—a powerful call resonating from the depths of the Guyanese rainforest. As Mary's eyes shone with resolve and appreciation for our time spent at home, she locked eyes with me, conveying a silent urgency. It was evident to us both: our journey was just beginning.

On the serene Webster porch, as I played cherished Southern tunes that evoked a sense of warmth and yearning, Mary looked at me and declared, "We must go back—to those in need of our support, to the essential tasks that lie before us." Her words struck a chord within us, sparking a passion that ignited our spirits.

Fueled by prayer and a sense of purpose, we set our course back to Guyana, strengthened by our belief in the significance of our mission. We could not overlook the need for our help; it was time to return and honor our commitment to those who were counting on us. We had no problem navigating the Essequibo River this time. It was smooth sailing.

Our adventure took us back to Moraikobal, a captivating village that greeted us with wonder and challenges. The lively chorus of the rainforest felt like the embrace of an old friend, its enigmatic depths beckoning us to explore. We arrived energized and ready to reconnect with the essential aspects of our work that have been intricately intertwined with the vibrant fabric of this remarkable land. In this untamed paradise, we sensed a powerful call to purpose and adventure just waiting to be discovered.

Mary's steadfast dedication to education evolved into a transformative vision for the indigenous children of Moraikobal. She saw the incredible potential in each child—a flicker she was intent on igniting into a vibrant blaze through the power of knowledge. With relentless commitment and inspiring grace, she embarked on the journey to create a new school for the village, a shining beacon of hope and opportunity.

While I watched, the men of the community, radiating strength and determination, began building an open-air pavilion crowned with a thatched roof. This simple yet meaningful structure, made from local materials and crafted through their combined efforts, was set to become the centerpiece of the new school. Inside its sun-drenched walls, Mary greeted a diverse assembly of enthusiastic students—children of all ages, united by their desire for knowledge and a hopeful future. We worked with our thirty-eight baptized youth and taught them more from the Word of God and watched as their spirits grew.

On even the most challenging days, when Mary grappled with creating lessons across a multitude of subjects in a single improvised classroom, her gentle persistence and bright smile lit the way to comprehension. She went beyond mere teaching; she inspired, connecting intricate ideas with eager young minds. Her solid dedication and passion for education were not merely lessons imparted but seeds sown, destined to nurture a brighter future for the children of Moraikobal and their community.

In our distinctive setting, my efforts evolved with a pragmatic emphasis that deeply connected with the everyday realities of the village women, who continually battled for survival. They turned to us, eager for simple solutions that could create real change. I dedicated myself to uplifting them by introducing new methods—one of which utilized the plentiful energy of the sun.

With easily obtainable materials, we created a DIY solar panel using aluminum foil and durable cardboard. This innovative device had a straightforward yet impactful purpose: it enabled the women to cook food more efficiently and sustainably. I built the inaugural oven for the community—a simple brick-and-mortar structure that stood as a symbol of creativity in our remote environment.

As this seed of potential began to flourish, the villagers felt inspired to construct more ovens, enthusiastically embracing the techniques I had shared. This joint endeavor not only improved their everyday lives but also sparked a sense of unity and innovation within the community, laying the foundation for a brighter and more sustainable future.

Fueled by a passion to make a meaningful difference, I turned my attention to another pressing issue: the urgent demand for clean, fresh water. The magnificent river that meandered past Moraikobal was not only a breathtaking natural landmark; it also represented an untapped resource brimming with potential. With the invaluable support of the local men, we worked together to devise an innovative strategy for harnessing its energy. We constructed a straightforward yet efficient system—a network of pulleys and channels—crafted to capture the river's energy and deliver purified water to each household in the village. Every drop of this water, meticulously filtered by the wisdom of nature and our combined creativity, serves as a powerful reminder of our steadfast dedication to improving the quality of life for everyone in our community.

As the blistering sun gave way to the soothing allure of warm, starlit nights, our community sprang to life beneath the welcoming radiance of the newly built pavilion. Three nights a week, the whole village gathered in a profound expression of worship, forming a vibrant tapestry of unity and faith. At the center of it all, I would sit with my guitar, strumming beloved hymns that intertwined the rich threads of our various cultures and histories.

The melodies would rise into the night, merging with our voices in a harmonious expression of hope—a tribute to faith, strength, and the enduring ties of community. Each note told our stories, and every song echoed a collective yearning for connection.

During those cherished moments, I enthusiastically embraced every chance to share Bible lessons with the women and children around me. Each parable and prayer transformed into meaningful conversations—tender reminders that our common humanity transcends all divisions. Together, we rejoiced in the abundance of our lives, cultivating seeds of understanding, compassion, and love that thrived within our community. This was not merely worship; it was a life-changing experience that united us, illuminating the journey of togetherness as we advanced side by side.

Our six years in Guyana were a transformative experience, marked by both challenges and meaningful triumphs. We returned to Georgia on two memorable occasions: first, to celebrate Brad's graduation from Georgia Tech, and later, to honor Penny's achievements at South University. Brad resumed his studies at Georgia Tech, fueled by a fervent desire to earn an engineering degree that would support his future work. He chose a path that combined intellectual depth with heartfelt compassion—qualities vital for making a lasting difference. Meanwhile, Penny's progress in nursing highlighted not only her innate ability to care for others but also the skills she honed through dedication and perseverance. Her development stands as a testament to her character and the invaluable lessons she had gained during our time in Cambodia and India.

Each journey back home reinforced our steadfast dedication to the mission we had once embarked upon. In Georgia, we relished the comforting warmth of family and the rich traditions that surrounded us. Yet, even in these moments of refuge, our hearts yearned for the raw authenticity of Guyana.

I often found myself reflecting on those peaceful afternoons by the river, where the sound of the flowing water blended beautifully with our sincere prayers. Mary's writings—rooted in the labor of challenging work and the excitement of change—tenderly captured our experiences, merging the craft of a poet with the commitment of a missionary. Her articles not only inspired but also served as a testament to the everyday miracles flourishing in a land so different from the comforts of home.

Looking back on our experiences in Guyana, it's evident that those years profoundly influenced us, much like the jungle shaped the land itself. The challenges of establishing a school, teaching vital skills in a place where nature reigned, and blending technology with ancient traditions forged an unbreakable bond between us and the people of Moraikobal. This connection goes beyond the limits of time. Each obstacle we overcame and every triumph we celebrated became ingrained in our being, serving as a testament to the hopeful promise of our shared journey—one that we aspire to pass on to future generations, encouraging them to uphold the legacy of resilience and potential.

As I stand on the aged wooden porch, surrounded by the gentle twilight and the refreshing breeze from the river, a profound realization washes over me: our time in Guyana was far more than just a brief chapter of our mission. It was a remarkable testament to the strength of human connection, the incredible power of faith, and the unyielding spirit of a community that refuses to let adversity define them.

In this wild, vibrant, and at times treacherous paradise, we found not just a calling, but a genuine home—a home that has woven itself into the fabric of our hearts, shaping our lives eternally. This experience has left an everlasting imprint on our souls, inspiring us to carry forward the lessons learned and the love shared, reminding us that together, we can overcome any obstacle.

CHAPTER TWELVE

New York Calling

After six exhilarating years in Moraikobal, fate revealed an exceptional opportunity when a letter arrived on a crisp autumn morning. Its embossed seal was unmistakable: an invitation for Mary to speak at the esteemed National Geographic Convention in New York City. Though the letter had lingered in our mailbox for two weeks, its message resonated like a clarion call, demanding our attention. Mary was not merely invited to highlight her breathtaking photographs and compelling stories of indigenous cultures; she would take the stage before a captivated audience; their gaze fixed on a massive screen displaying vivid snapshots of our remarkable journey. This was the moment Mary had eagerly anticipated—a chance to share the essence of our remote lands with the world. As I read her acceptance, a surge of exhilaration washed over me, filling me with immense pride and excitement. This was more than just an invitation; it was a transformative opportunity that could alter the course of our lives forever.

Before embarking on our next adventure, I urgently contacted the bishop in Georgetown. I let him know about our upcoming departure and formally requested the customary six-week furlough. With our children now adults and beginning their lives outside of their respective schools, we felt it was time to go home. We made the decision for the entire family to journey to New York together. The prospect of immersing ourselves in the vibrant, soaring skyline filled us with a mix of excitement and nervous energy, fully aware that this experience would profoundly impact our family.

The journey from Guyana was a thrilling roller-coaster of emotions and meticulous planning that will forever be etched in my memory. As I took my seat next to Mary on the small commuter flight, an electrifying tension buzzed through the cabin. In that close moment, we shared a knowing look that seemed to silently say, "We're truly embarking on this adventure."

As the plane neared New York, the skyline gradually unveiled itself against the glowing horizon, crafting a stunning scene reminiscent of a movie. Touching down in New York City was a remarkable feast for the senses. Both of our children would arrive on a later flight, and we would greet them.

New York thrummed with energy: car horns created a frenetic symphony, the voices of diverse crowds intertwined like a rich tapestry, and neon signs twinkled like contemporary stars against the night. The rhythmic rumbles of the subway resonated with the hopes of countless dreamers, all eager to chase their aspirations. It was a vibrant illustration of the endless opportunities that awaited us in this dynamic metropolis.

In the thrilling days leading up to the convention, New York City morphed into both our playground and our stage for adventure. Mary, the kids, and I zipped through the vibrant chaos of Times Square, relishing the excitement of getting lost in the intricate maze of subway stations—where the soft patter of rain against the glass transformed the ordinary into a radiant kaleidoscope. We escaped to peaceful nooks in Central Park, cherishing brief moments of tranquility to center ourselves and soak in the city's relentless energy. In every lively street and quiet corner, we discovered inspiration that ignited our enthusiasm for the events ahead.

The day of Mary's speech had arrived, a moment that felt like it was frozen in time. Backstage, in a dim corridor behind the grand hall, Mary sat in front of a mirror, her reflection revealing a blend of resolve and anxiety. Her hands trembled as she flipped through her carefully annotated notes. I observed her pacing, the electric vibe of the convention hall pulsing through the thick curtains. In that critical, tense moment, she clutched a crumpled letter from a loyal supporter—a poignant reminder of the obstacles she had conquered to stand here today. Taking a deep breath, she summoned her strength, prepared to channel her nerves into a powerful message that would resonate with everyone in attendance.

As Mary stepped onto the stage, an unexpected glitch disrupted the once lively ambiance: the projected images froze on a stark, dark screen, and an eerie silence enveloped the speakers. Gasps and whispers rippled through the audience like wildfire. For a moment, time seemed to halt. Yet, in that pivotal instant, Mary displayed remarkable strength. She discarded her notes, took a deep breath, and spoke from the heart—raw and unfiltered. Her voice carried a powerful authenticity, captivating the crowd with the genuine essence of her firsthand experiences. Each word she uttered felt like a revelation, pulling everyone into her narrative.

While the technical team raced against time to fix the visuals, her powerful message captivated the audience. When her photographs finally lit up the screen, a surge of applause filled the room—an exhilarating standing ovation that highlighted the importance of their collective journey. In that instant, every risk they had taken was justified; the bond they shared was both tangible and deeply meaningful. Both children thoroughly enjoyed her presentation and felt proud of what their mother had accomplished.

Following the event, New York enveloped us in a vibrant array of experiences. We roamed the lively streets, skillfully dodging the iconic yellow cabs while immersing ourselves in the energetic atmosphere brought to life by street performers and eye-catching public art. Mary found herself spontaneously interviewing respected cultural editors, her reflections vividly encapsulating the spirit of our exciting adventures and the complex tapestry of global humanity. At the same time, I was engaged in stimulating conversations with local community leaders in cozy coffee shops, where the dynamic flow of ideas underscored a powerful truth: every nook of this extraordinary city brims with limitless possibilities.

Amid the joyful whirlwind that enveloped us, our family found cherished pockets of tranquility. Nestled in a peaceful spot within a bustling park, I sat with Brad and Penny, who are growing into insightful and self-reliant young adults. As we shared stories about their dreams and the lessons they've picked up in school back home, I was impressed by their maturity and the charming flashes of youthful wit. It became evident that, regardless of the miles we've traveled, the unshakeable bond of family remains our firm foundation.

The turning point in our transition came soon after. When I returned to Georgia, I found an official summons from Mission Headquarters in Atlanta waiting for me, leading me into a grand, wood-paneled conference room. Inside, a group of experienced missionaries—committed colleagues who had fervently supported our cause for many years—were gathered, their expressions keen with determination. The air was thick with expectation as they discussed the future of our ministry, wrestling with vital questions that delved into the core of our vision. I was invited by the group to take the reins as the Executive Director of Missions in Atlanta.

As my moment approached, a deep silence settled over the room. Questions flew at me from all sides, yet within the chaos, a steadfast certainty welled up inside me. Fueled by a clear understanding rooted in my dedication to our mission, I confidently proclaimed, "Yes—I accept the position of Executive Director in Atlanta!" In that pivotal instant, as approving nods and warm smiles spread across the room, I understood that our journey was not merely progressing; it was taking off to new heights.

Before fully stepping into my new leadership role, I had the invaluable opportunity to return to Guyana for two weeks. This time was essential for me to meet the new missionary who would be leading our beloved initiatives and to ensure a seamless transition for the programs we had nurtured in the Moraikobal community.

My visit was filled with a whirlwind of emotions—a heartfelt mixture of bittersweet goodbyes and sincere assurances that our mission would not only continue but thrive in our absence. Surrounded by the sounds of the rainforest and the familiar rhythms of life in Guyana, I took a moment to cherish the vibrant faces that had become so precious to us, reinforcing my deep conviction in the lasting impact of our work.

As I find myself on the threshold of this transformative journey, the dazzling lights of Times Square and the underlying rhythm of the subway serve as a reminder that our purpose is limitless. The relentless energy of New York has sparked a deep courage within us and a spirit of innovation, revitalizing our commitment to the mission that has inspired us for so long. From the historic roads of Guyana to the vibrant heart of America's urban landscape, we are propelled by an unyielding dedication to our cause. In this moment, we wholeheartedly embrace the endless possibilities that lie ahead.

As Mary's voice gains traction on national stages and our children grow increasingly insightful and empathetic, I feel a deep sense of purpose. Our journey—encompassing adventures in vast wildernesses and lively urban landscapes—serves as a strong testament to resilience, hope, and the transformative power of storytelling. With the city lights sparkling in the distance, I am certain that we are on the brink of an even brighter future.

Chapter Thirteen

Back in Georgia

As I returned from Guyana to Webster, it felt as though the worries from the distant jungles melted away beneath the welcoming Southern skies. I disembarked in Savannah, and immediately spotted Mary and our parents brimming with joy as we stood there in the terminal, eager to embrace me back home. Just an hour later, we found ourselves driving into the familiar warmth of Webster, where the humid air enveloped us like a long-lost hug, infused with the inviting aroma of freshly cut grass and the nostalgic echoes of our childhood escapades. This homecoming was more than a simple return; it signified a meaningful transition as we bid farewell to our travels—from the wild landscapes of Guyana to the vibrant pulse of New York—and stepped into a realm filled with beloved memories and the thrilling potential of new beginnings.

Upon my return to my family home, I was taken aback by the extraordinary journey Mary had undertaken in my absence. While I was busy traversing perilous rivers and crafting innovative solutions in distant villages, she was flourishing as a captivating storyteller and speaker. Numerous speaking invitations flooded in, each offering her a chance to share our inspiring stories of hope, resilience, and transformation with audiences across the country.

One moment stands out clearly in my mind—reading one of her emails aloud. Her words were so richly detailed that the distant landscapes we had explored sprang to life around us. Her articles were not mere travel accounts; they were powerful narratives filled with raw honesty and accompanied by stunning photographs. They served as windows into the hearts of the people we met, demonstrating how love and service can bridge even the greatest divides. Through her storytelling, Mary wasn't just narrating our adventures; she was shedding light on the universal truths of human connection and the profound influence we can have in each other's lives. Her work is more than just inspirational; it's a powerful reminder of how storytelling can cultivate empathy and understanding in an increasingly divided world. I still picture her as that captivating and vibrant young sixteen-year-old I first met in Webster and immediately fell in love with.

Shortly after I returned, Mary and I were excited to begin the next chapter of our lives. We decided to settle in Buckhead, a charming area of Atlanta, conveniently located just minutes from the mission headquarters where I would assume my new role as executive director. The shift from field missionary to a leadership position in a vibrant urban ministry was both thrilling and daunting. My days were filled with intense strategy sessions, impactful board meetings, and meaningful conversations with experienced missionaries, all looking to me for guidance. Each meeting highlighted the wealth of experience I had acquired abroad and the significant responsibility I now bore in nurturing a global mission network. My vision was clear: to turn our hard-won lessons into a strong framework that would not only support but also enhance our mission's work worldwide. Leading and inspiring change was more than just a job; it was a calling, and I was eager to embrace it with enthusiasm and purpose.

At home, our new life flourished within the enchanting rhythms of Southern living. Our Buckhead abode exuded warmth and hospitality, blending the vibrant pulse of Atlanta with the soothing embrace of suburban peace. Each evening, after navigating a long day of meetings, I would retreat to our porch, enchanted by the gentle twilight settling over the city. With my guitar cradled in my hands, I strummed familiar melodies that whisked me back to simpler times, even as dreams for the future swirled in my mind. Mary sat beside me, her eyes gleaming with her own aspirations. Her speaking engagements and articles were more than just career milestones; they were heartfelt missions to transform our shared experiences into compelling stories meant to inspire and uplift others.

Our children, Brad and Penny, have graduated from college with outstanding achievements, and coming back to Georgia has provided a fantastic chance to reconnect. I truly value the late-night talks I have with Brad, where he fervently debates social justice topics, innovative engineering, and the essential importance of community. Witnessing his transformation from a carefree child adventuring through wild jungles to a young man with an intense sense of purpose fills me with immense pride.

Penny is a source of immense pride as she thrives in her first nursing role at the Medical Center in Macon, just a couple of hours away. Her journey brings our family pure joy and inspiration. During our cozy family dinners at our favorite local restaurants and leisurely afternoons at the park, Penny enthusiastically recounts her experiences from her clinical rotations. Her passion and unwavering dedication to caring for others embody the compassion that has long been a cornerstone of our family values. Brad and Penny are not just our children; they are living testaments to love in action, making a significant impact on those around them.

Weekends became cherished moments—an array of meaningful traditions that grounded our new life in Georgia. We wholeheartedly embraced the simplicity and charm of local living, exploring vibrant neighborhoods, joining community events, and even hosting impromptu family reunions that filled our home with laughter, joy, and the warmth of shared memories. As I looked around our living room, adorned with Mary's latest framed photographs of our adventures next to cherished keepsakes from our past, a comforting realization washed over me. These visual reminders represented that, no matter how far our journey had taken us, our roots remained steadfast and solid.

As I took on the exhilarating challenge of leading a global mission, I experienced a deep sense of humility and gratitude woven into each moment of our extraordinary journey. Every strategic meeting in the lively, glass-walled boardrooms of Atlanta and each enlightening discussion with my committed colleagues echoed the whispers of remote villages, the rustling of untamed forests, and the sincere prayers from far-off lands. I recognized that our story—filled with obstacles, revelations, and meaningful human connections—had only grown richer and broader over time, transforming into a source of inspiration that propels us forward as one.

As I pen these thoughts on this tranquil Georgia evening, I am struck by the deep realization that our narrative is still in progress. With steadfast faith, the unshakeable backing of family and community, and the uplifting words of Mary echoing far beyond their initial context, I gaze toward the future with steadfast hope. The journey that began on Hickory Street has taken us through vibrant jungles, expansive oceans, and towering cityscapes, ultimately bringing us back home. Yet it also lays a robust foundation for crafting even bolder and more transformative chapters to come. Together, we hold the power to shape a brighter future filled with endless possibilities.

Chapter Fourteen

Retirement

The long-awaited moment came when I realized that the frantic pace of missions, crises, and breakthroughs was giving way to something deeply transformative—a calm and unhurried rhythm. My retirement wasn't merely a sudden farewell; it was a gradual, soul-enriching evolution. After years spent navigating the jungles of Guyana and Cambodia, India, and Suriname; leading high-stakes meetings in New York; and nurturing growth in communities back in Georgia, I arrived at a remarkable crossroads where the essence of my past elegantly merged with the promise of my future, all encapsulated in a quiet yet illuminating moment of clarity.

That morning is etched in my memory with remarkable clarity. The atmosphere buzzed with energy, almost buoyant, as I sat in my office for the last
time, surrounded by colleagues who had become dear
friends over the years. A rush of pride swept over me,
mingling with nostalgia and a palpable excitement for
what lay ahead. Their heartfelt words and genuine
expressions reflected the legacy we had built together—one forged through dedication, compassion, and
an unwavering belief in our mission. In that poignant
moment, the challenges I encountered while leading
a global endeavor transformed into treasured memories, resonating softly like a gentle breeze beneath the
magnolia trees of my childhood, a testament to the
profound journey we had shared.

As I made my way back to Buckhead after the official retirement ceremony, I wandered thoughtfully through our familiar streets, relishing the soothing
pace of a life now free from the burdens of deadlines
and crisis meetings. At our front door, Mary welcomed me with a beaming smile—one that celebrated our shared journey and hinted at the exciting new
adventures awaiting us. While these adventures may
be quieter, I know they will be just as fulfilling and
significant. That evening, we settled onto the porch,

where the final rays of sunlight blended with the soft sounds of the neighborhood. With my guitar in hand, I began to play, allowing each note to transform into a heartfelt expression of gratitude. Each chord resonated with memories of far-off places, the obstacles we had overcome, and the lives we had impacted along the way. This moment marked not just the close of one chapter but the thrilling start of another, brimming with promise and purpose.

Embracing retirement signified not only a fresh chapter in my life but also a significant transformation towards a more intentional and gratifying rhythm. I began to appreciate the joy of cherishing moments that had previously slipped away amid the relentless demands of our mission. The extended, tranquil hours evolved into my refuge as I delved into old journals—a vibrant collection of letters, photographs, and weathered sketches that elegantly chronicled our numerous adventures.

These treasured artifacts whisked me away into a realm of memories, often bringing me back to spirited discussions in a small Guyanese village or the vibrant energy of New York's lively streets. Each memory surfaced like a jewel, shining light on the zeal that once drove my journey—a passion that still radiates gently within me. In this more subdued chapter of life, I have come to understand that these memories are not just echoes of the past; rather, they are invaluable treasures that inspire and nourish my spirit, encouraging me to contemplate a life richly lived.

For me, retirement wasn't about disengaging; it was about evolving my role into something even more meaningful. Rather than leaving the mission behind, I seized the chance to mentor and guide the next generation of missionaries. I opened my home and local community centers to facilitate regular gatherings, where I could share the wealth of stories and lessons I've accumulated from decades of global adventures. I would be invited to speak at numerous churches across the Southeast for missions. The work continues.

On those cozy afternoons, sipping sweet tea, I listened attentively to aspiring missionaries as they courageously opened up about their dreams and doubts. Whenever they turned to me for guidance, I would stress that genuine service is not just a fleeting phase, but a lifelong dedication—a sacred torch that is carefully passed from one individual to another. Each of these conversations brought me great satisfaction, as I understood that even in taking a step back, my own experiences would continue to inspire and motivate others, illuminating their journeys with the lessons of the past.

Mary, a powerful figure in the realm of storytelling, has launched into an exciting new phase of her remarkable career, exuding fresh energy and passion. Her speaking engagements have soared to new levels, now elegantly paired with a collection of deeply introspective writings that reflect the profound beauty of a life committed to service. In her prose, she paints a vivid picture of the tranquil peace found on our Buckhead porch, the joyful laughter that resonates throughout our home during shared meals, and the meaningful conversations that connect our past experiences to our hopeful future.

Her writings, filled with vibrant detail and heartfelt emotion, echo the essence of memoirs—a profound narrative that captures not only our travels but also a transformative journey toward spiritual and personal growth. Watching her skillfully intertwine our shared experiences into every sentence fills me with immense pride. I view our retirement as more than simply a break; it is a celebration of our continuing story, where each soft whisper adds depth to the rich narrative instead of being overshadowed by loud declarations. Mary's work not only pays tribute to our past but also inspires everyone who engages with it, making this chapter one of the most captivating yet.

Our children, Brad and Penny, have grown into extraordinary adults, each passionately forging their own distinct paths. Brad is excelling at Georgia Power, where he is involved in groundbreaking engineering projects that reflect the essence of our global adventures—initiatives focused on sustainable solutions designed to uplift and transform local communities. At the same time, Penny is thriving in her nursing career, sharing inspiring stories from her clinical experiences, driven by a combination of compassion and steadfast determination that fills me with both pride and comfort. Their achievements stand as a vibrant testament to the values we've instilled in them over the years, reminding me that as I step back from active leadership, our mission is much larger than myself. It represents a continuous journey of growth and evolution, now entrusted to the next generation, who are moving it forward with their own vision and purpose.

Penny married a former classmate from South University who is originally from Dahlonega, and together they have created a lovely family with a son and a daughter. Driven by her passion for healthcare, she has taken on the prestigious position of head nurse at North Georgia Medical Center, where she is making a meaningful difference in the lives of her patients and the community.

Brad discovered love with a captivating and lovely young woman from Macon, and together they have created a beautiful life. As the plant manager at Georgia Power's Riverside facility in Macon, Brad takes great pride in his significant role, overseeing the smooth and efficient operation of the plant. The couple is fortunate to have a wonderful daughter, and their family is flourishing, reaping the rewards of their hard work and commitment to each other.

In our retirement, Mary and I embraced moments of pure joy that truly enhanced our lives. Imagine us sharing a delightful weekend picnic in a nearby park, where we entertained our grandchildren with tales of our past escapades—each story sparking laughter and strengthening our connection. Picture quiet drives along scenic country roads, the radio softly playing nostalgic melodies that transported us back to treasured memories. These simple joys captured the true spirit of retirement: a precious opportunity to reconnect not only with each other but also with our family and the enduring beauty of life's everyday moments. This stage of life isn't merely about slowing down; it's about cherishing each moment and deepening our relationships with the people we hold most dear.

As I reflect on this peaceful autumn evening, I find myself filled with deep gratitude. Retirement has not simply marked a conclusion; it has been a journey of transformation—one that lets me savor the fruits of a lifetime of challenging work. It provides me with the opportunity to cultivate cherished connections made across faraway places and to share the inspiration that has driven my life's purpose.

As I contemplate the meandering journeys that have brought me to this point, I am filled with wonder at the adventures I have experienced—ranging from the wild, resonant calls of the jungle to the lively, energetic streets of New York, and now to a serene life, beautifully intertwined with treasured moments and love. This transformation isn't solely about what I have let go; it's about welcoming the glorious opportunities that lie ahead, brimming with purpose and connection.

As the gentle twilight envelops the evening sky and the stars start to shine, I feel a deep sense of comfort in this phase of retirement—not as a farewell, but as an invitation to embrace new beginnings. Though my voice may now be softer, it still carries the same steadfast conviction that once resonated around the world. Love, faith, and service are eternal, and our lives weave a colorful tapestry of hope that keeps on unfolding. This is not the conclusion of my journey; rather, it signifies the commencement of a new adventure rich with purpose and potential.

CHAPTER FIFTEEN

The Final Goodbye

I can still clearly remember the soft yet deeply moving words spoken by Dr. Hodges in that serene hospital hallway:

"It is with a great deal of sadness that I must convey this message, Mrs. Brown. Regrettably, it seems that Harold will not recover this time."

In that overwhelming moment, the sterile walls felt as though they were closing in on me, intensifying my despair. My heart, weary and battered from our years of shared challenges, felt like it might break apart. Yet, even in the depths of my pain, I found a wellspring of strength within myself. I understood that I needed to remain steadfast—not only for Harold, but for the deep love that has been the foundation of our vibrant life together. This love deserves my perseverance, and I won't allow hardship to eclipse the extraordinary journey we've created together.

Taking a deep breath, I entered his room, my heart brimming with resolve. The warm sunlight streamed through the window, bathing his peaceful face in a golden hue. Even though Harold lay unresponsive, I instinctively reached for his familiar hand, hoping that this small gesture could tether the treasured memories of our past and keep them from fading into oblivion.

"Harold," I murmured softly, wrapping my words in warmth and comfort. "I'm right here by your side, my love. You're not alone in this."

I settled into the chair beside his bed, resolved to create a vibrant tapestry of our treasured memories. I recalled our first dance beneath a sky adorned with twinkling lights, where every step felt enchanting. I reminisced about the tranquil evenings we spent wrapped in each other's embrace, as the world outside faded away, along with the thrilling adventures we embarked on in far-off places, each moment a testament to our connection. With each story, I sought not just to break the silence but to help him feel the rhythm of our laughter and the echoes of our dreams, hoping each word would reach him wherever he might be.

In that solemn watch, time appeared to stretch into a personal eternity. Surrounded by the soft beeping of the machines and the constant reminder of life's fragility, I took a moment to reflect on the cherished moments we've experienced together. He has been my steadfast compass through life's challenges, and our shared faith has brightened even the darkest days. I reminisced about the subtle, everyday miracles that have intricately bound our wonderfully complex life. Every word I uttered felt like a sincere prayer—a profound hope that our love would gently guide him into the next phase of existence.

As the evening light enveloped the room in a gentle, muted gold, I watched him intently, observing how his breathing became increasingly deep, each exhale a significant release. With the utmost care, I leaned down to plant a soft kiss on his forehead, murmuring, "I love you, forever." In that brief moment, I sensed his warmth beginning to diminish, as though the very essence of him was being whisked away by the soft evening breeze. Then, in that sacred stillness, Harold slipped away, leaving behind a silence that felt both agonizing and sacred, a testament to the love we had shared.

In the days that followed, I was wrapped in a bittersweet mix of grief and gratitude. At his funeral, I faced a gathering in our cherished local church—a space that became a haven of light, illuminated by the colorful rays streaming through the stained-glass windows. Friends, family, and even those I didn't know joined together to pay tribute to a man whose kindness echoed everywhere, from the bustling streets of New York to the tranquil jungles of Guyana.

As I spoke, I felt the profound impact of his legacy in every word. I reflected on his steadfast guidance, his genuine dedication to helping others, and the multitude of small yet significant moments that highlighted his extraordinary life. I recalled the way he patiently taught Brad to ride a bike, nurturing his confidence with each gentle lesson. I conveyed the warmth that enveloped our home every time his signature smile lit up the room. His spirit and love lifted everyone who knew him, and we came together not only to grieve his passing but to honor a life truly well-lived—one that made a meaningful difference.

As the ethereal notes of "Amazing Grace" filled the air, sung beautifully a cappella by a beloved friend, I was struck by a deep revelation: although Harold has departed from this world, his spirit continues to shine brilliantly through the lives he touched. In that sacred moment, I found myself wrapped in a rich mosaic of memories—resounding laughter, shared tears, and the unwavering hope of a love that defies time. Harold's essence remains with us, serving as a poignant reminder that even though he is no longer physically present, his legacy of love and kindness endures in our hearts, guiding us on our journeys ahead.

Returning home was a profoundly somber yet transformative experience. During peaceful afternoons in our cherished garden, I would be enveloped by the familiar aroma of freshly cut grass and the gentle rustling of magnolia leaves. It was here that I took a moment to reflect. As I flipped through old journals and traced my fingers over treasured photographs, I found comfort in the memories—each vibrant moment of our shared journey serving as a soothing balm for my aching heart. In those quiet hours alone, I came to understand that every tear I shed and every smile that appeared was not merely a remembrance but a heartfelt homage to the remarkable legacy Harold left behind. These reflections transcended loss; they were a celebration of a life that deeply influenced mine and the enduring impact he continues to have within me.

As night wraps the world in its embrace and the gentle whispers of cherished memories flood my mind, I face the future with an open and heartfelt acceptance. This final goodbye is not just an end; it signifies a journey of transformation. It symbolizes the gentle passing of a torch—a lasting reminder that the love we shared, the stories we created, and the lives we impacted will forever illuminate my path. With Harold's voice echoing warmly in my heart, I am prepared to move forward into a life that honors his legacy and transforms grief into resilience. Together, we embarked on a journey of love, and now, I will carry that legacy forward, driven by the strength of our shared moments.

As the first rays of dawn emerge, I gently voice my last goodbye—not as a conclusion, but as a sincere promise that our love will endure, transcending the bounds of time and space. It's a commitment that no distance or situation can weaken the profound bond between us.

Epilogue

I n the serene moments after a life filled with adventures and challenges, I am overwhelmed by a
deep sense of gratitude. This feeling is more than just
a momentary emotion; it is profound and lasting, a
reflection of a love-driven mission that has illuminated our journey at every step. My heart is filled with
thankfulness for each person who has responded to
the call to serve. To every courageous individual who
has stepped into the world of missions, bringing with
them courage, compassion, and a steadfast commitment to deliver hope to those who need it most—I
extend my heartfelt thanks. Your devotion has not
only inspired those around you, but it has also ignited
a transformative power capable of changing lives and
communities. Together, we shine as beacons of light,
creating a meaningful impact in the world.

I have personally witnessed the deep and lasting effects of service. Imagine a child's joyful smile in a remote village, a quiet nod of gratitude amid urban hustle, or a heartfelt letter from someone whose life was transformed by a simple act of kindness. These touching moments remind us that the purpose of service goes beyond individual experiences; it echoes through every act of selflessness, every endeavor to connect across cultures, and every hopeful prayer for a better tomorrow. Each of these actions sends out ripples that extend well beyond their immediate effects, highlighting the essential nature of our work. Together, we can inspire change and create a lasting tapestry of hope for future generations.

To all who have embraced this noble mission: recognize that your commitment and sacrifices form the very essence of a transformative movement without limits. Your bravery in exploring the unfamiliar, confronting the challenges of uncharted landscapes, and wholeheartedly serving others is nothing short of remarkable. Whether you are kindling hope in remote jungles, engaging with community members in lively urban centers, or sharing impactful stories through your writing that resonate worldwide, you are a vital part of an unyielding chain of service and love that reverberates through the ages. Together, we are crafting a legacy that will inspire future generations.

As we arrive at these closing thoughts, I invite you to understand that no gesture of kindness is too minor to create an impact. Each of us carry a distinctive spark—an ember that has fueled our journeys from Cambodia to Guyana, from the dynamic heartbeat of New York City to the welcoming warmth of Southern hospitality. When this spark is nurtured by faith and propelled by love, it holds the remarkable potential to illuminate even the bleakest areas of our world. Embrace this strength, for together, we can generate a ripple of compassion that extends well beyond ourselves.

May you discover profound satisfaction in realizing that each moment you dedicate to serving others contributes a crucial strand to the beautiful tapestry of God's kingdom. As you persist in your mission—whether facing challenges on the frontlines or finding peace in prayer—may you feel the warm embrace of a legacy that reaches beyond time. Keep in mind that your sacrifices are not losses, but rather potent seeds sown in rich soil, ready to thrive and yield fruit long after the present fades away. Embrace this journey with the confidence that your dedication is creating a brighter future for the generations that follow.

As I wrap up this narrative, my heart is filled with hope and my spirit remains resolute, driven by the dedication of numerous generations of devoted servants. Our path has been fraught with challenges and bittersweet goodbyes, but it is also brightly lit by the possibility of new beginnings and the enduring power of love. Let the legacy of service and hope serve as your guiding beacon, and know that I will continue to nurture that flame, shining a light for all who are courageous enough to answer this noble call. Together, we can motivate and uplift those who come after us.

With steadfast love and sincere gratitude,

Mary

About the Author

The Rev. Dr. Charles E. Cravey, a prolific author of forty-six books spanning novels, novellas, poetry, devotionals, and Bible studies, has long captivated readers with his insightful and inspiring writing. His works are widely admired, earning him multiple **Publisher's Choice Awards** throughout his career.

This book weaves together a narrative drawn from Dr. Cravey's remarkable sixty-eight foreign mission trips, shaped by his leadership in guiding teams across France, Spain, Guyana, Venezuela, Ecuador, the Caribbean, and every country in Central America. His dedication to missions has sparked a new generation of servants devoted to God and the church, embodying his deep understanding of both the calling and the journey.

Now retired from full-time ministry with The United Methodist Church, Dr. Cravey resides in Statesboro, Georgia, with his wife, Renee. They are blessed with two children and two grandchildren, all continuing to make a meaningful impact on the world.

OTHER BOOKS BY DR. CRAVEY MAY BE FOUND AT:

https://drcharlescravey.com or by ordering from Amazon, Books a Million, or wherever you purchase books.